Taxi Land

I was forty two years old when I began driving a taxi.

I had taken early retirement from the military, and although driving a taxi hadn't originally been a part of my plans for my so called golden years, it ended up that way regardless.

I had always been a dream of mine to buy a car, fix it up, and just drive *everywhere*, all over the country, and see things I'd never see in the big city. As it turned out, though, the farthest I'd driven was to the next county over.

But, I was making some extra cash, enjoying driving around, meeting new people, and even making a new friend here and there.

But, believe me, driving a taxi – especially at night – can also be very dangerous.

#

One would think that driving a taxi at night would be excting and interesting, which it could be, yes. But driving a taxi, you don't always know exactly who might call for a ride.

For example, you have your drunks who, while observing a much safer way to get home instead of drving while intoxicated, can still be loud, obnoxious, and even downright mean.

Another example of your average taxi never knowing who {or what} he might run into next, is the night I picked up Billy Hankins.

Billy was a young fella from the North end of town, who was doing weekends at the county jail as opposed to doing straight time.

In the North end of town, drugs, alcohol, burglary, arson, street fighting, and bar brawling was the norm on any given day. Residents were in fear of their safety after dark – and at times even during the daytime hours. In the North end you either belonged or you didn't and if you didn't, you didn't come in less you got your ass whipped.

Street toughs ruled their corner of the block, and dared any "outsider" to cross their turf. A trip to the store for a loaf of bread was considered an act of bravery.

But somehow, Billy had come out of this hell hole smelling like a rose compared to some of his old buddies, and was even planning on studying for his GED diploma in the near future.

That is, if he could manage not to screw it up.

That night, as I picked him up to deliver him to the county jail, he seemed sort of nervous, fidgety, and didn't have nuch to say. Considering where he was going, I didn't blame him.

As we pulled away from his apartment building, I could see through my rearview mirror that he kept fidgeting with something behind his back and making strange, moaning sounds, as though he was in pain.

Coming to a stoplight ahead, I said, "Are you alright, Billy boy? You seem as nervous as a whore in Church."

He forced a smile and said, "It's cool, Milo. I got some lower back pain, that's all."

I said, "I got some aspirin in the glove box."

He said, "No thanks, I'll be fine."

I said, "Back trouble is a bitch. Take it from me. Are you sure?"

He said, adamantly, "I said, *no*, but thanks."

The light changed and off we went. About two blocks up the street, he started moving around back there again, and making that weird moaning sound. I glanced up in my mirror to see his face was now literally contorted into a rictus of pain and agony, his right hand behind his back.

I pulled over, placed the gearshift in park, leaned over the back seat, and said, "Billy, what in the hell *are* you doing back there?"

His forehead bathed in sweat, he said, "Like I told you, old school, don't worry about it."

I said, "When you ride in *my* cab, I have to worry about it. I'll be legally liable for anything that happens to you."

With his right hand still behind his back, he said, "I said, don't *worry* about it."

I said, "Billy, I may be old school, but I'm not stupid. I know you young punks sneak shit into the jail. Now, what are you up to?"

Billy exposed his right hand to me. He was holding a very small piece of thin plastic, like a piece of a sandwich bag, filled with what looked like tobacco.

I said, "Yeah, so?"

His face flushed, he said, "I'm sneaking this in, if you must know."

I said, "Okay, but why is sneaking that into the

jail so painful for you?”

He said, embarrassingly, “I'm trying to cram it up my ass.”

I said, “Say what?! Are you nuts?”

He said, “They always check your pockets when you log in, and this way, they won't find it.”

Shaking my head in disbelief, I said, “Billy boy, have you ever heard of a strip search? Or a cavity search?”

He said, “I know that, Milo. But I need my tobacco, I really do. I mean, what would you do?”

Lighting a cigarette, I said, “I sure wouldn't be cramming tobacco up my ass, that's for sure.”

He said, jokingly, “No, you'd be cramming a can of beer up your ass, right?”

I couldn't argue with that. I said, “Okay, Billy boy. But do me a favor. Just get it done. My own ass is starting to hurt just thinking about it.”

With that, off we went again, toward the county jail.

A few minutes later, with his tobacco stash now tucked away firmly up his behind, we pulled up to the jail parking lot. As he climbed out, he said, “I owe you one, Milo. I'll pay you on Friday. Cool?”

I said, “Sure, kid. I know the drill.”

As he walked away, I couldn't help but be reminded of my own youth, and the stupid shit I used to do, too.

Except for cramming foreign objects up my butt, that is.

#

About half an hour later, as I cruised the North end for any other potential customers – folks who were too drunk to walk home from the tavern, druggies too high to find their own ass if it was right in front of them, etc. - was when I spotted old Miss Edwards, one of the local retirees, slowly pushing her scooter down the street, huffing and puffing and having a hard time.

I immediately pulled over, rolled down my window, and said, "Miss Edwards? You need a hand?"

She looked up at me with those old tired eyes, and said, "Oh, Milo. Thank God."

I said, jokingly, "I see that scooter you took from Walmart has failed you again."

She ssaid, jokingly, "Why don't you just say that a little louder, Milo? I don't think the folks over in the next county heard you."

I put the cab in park, climbed out, and looked the scooter over and said, "It's the battery, Margie. I told you that you needed to recharge it now and then."

She said, "Oh yeah, sure. I'll just push it out to Walmart and ask them to charge it for me."

I said, "Smartass."

She said, "Well? Are you just gonna stand there and giggle like a school boy, or are you gonna help me get this piece of crap home?"

I said, "It would be my pleasure."

#

It wasn't just like that in the North end, either.

It was like that all over town, and all over the country, by the year 2022.

I saw it every night almost, older folks just trying to get by, and more often than not, doing just that, *barely* getting by.

I couldn't blame them for being desperate enough to "borrow" a scooter either. Not that I condoned thievery, mind you, but I didn't condone watching our own government robbing us blind, either.

So, as far as I was concerned, Miss Edwards was now the defacto owner of a brand new Walmart scooter.

#

So, on I went, into the night, anxiously awaiting yet another exciting adventure.

As usual, I didn't have to wait long.

As I approached the corner of Second Street and St Clair, there she was – *whoever* she was – standing on the corner, waving me down, wanting a ride.

She was buck naked.

She was tall, lean, and had flame red hair and huge green eyes, and her skin was so *pale*, it seemed to shine like a beacon in the semi darkness of the street lights.

Yes, I was quite sure she needed a ride.

As I did a u-turn and pulled up to the corner, she leaned down and said through the window, "Please, mister. I *really* need a ride."

Her breath was even stronger than her body odor, both reeking of cheap booze. I said, "Yes, I'd say you most definitely need a ride. Hop in the back before the cops see you."

After she climbed into the back seat, I started driving South, *away* from the North end of town, figuring I'd seen enough North end action for one night.

As we headed out of the North side, she said, "Thank God! I had to get out of there."

I said, "May I ask you a personal question?"

She lit a cigarette and said, "Sure, go for it." Considering she wasn't wearing any clothes, I wasn't sure where she'd stashed a smoke and a lighter, and didn't really want to know, either.

I said, "Why are you walking around the North end buck naked?"

She took a drag from her cigarette and said, "It's a *long* story."

I said, "I figured that much already."

She said, "Then why did you ask?"

I said, "Well, it's not very often I see a good looking red head, buck naked, standing on a corner in the North end at night. It seemed a little odd, that's all."

She said, "I can understand that."

I said, "That doesn't answer my question."

She said, "Are you sure you want to hear it? It might take a while."

I said, "I wouldn't have asked otherwise."

She said, "Okay, but don't say I didn't warn you."

I said, "Just tell me the story. I'm falling asleep from boredom."

She said, "I was at a keg party, and we were playing strip poker, and-"

I said, "When I was your age, we called it playing "spin the bottle."

She said, "Cool. Anyway, we were playing strip

poker, and I was losing big time."

I said, with a grin, "That's obvious."

She said, "Anyway, mister smartass, I was at this party, and the cops raided it."

I said, "They must have really enjoyed arresting you, Miss Lady Godiva."

She said, "They didn't get the chance. I took off running out the back door, down the alley, and down to the tavern on the corner, to see if I could hitch a ride."

I said, "I bet you caught the attention of the men in there."

She said, "You bet I did. Some of them asked me to dance on the bar for tips."

I said, "I bet they did."

She said, "So, I thought, well, the whole night has been a bust, so I might as well make some money for cab fare."

I said, jokingly, "I bet you had enough money to buy a Greyhound bus."

Her face flushed as she said, "Aw...thank you."

I said, "Then what happened?"

She said, Then, the owner of the place walks in, and tells me to get out, that he's not going to jail for me dancing underage."

I said, "Oops. How old are you?"

She said, "Twenty five."

I said, "You're almost a minor, then. Speaking of which, I have some old blue jeans and a shirt in the trunk. I think you should get dressed for now."

She said, "Oh yes, please."

I pulled the cab over next to an empty parking lot, away from the street lights, and shut off the engine. I said, "And stay *inside* the cab, out of sight."

She flashed me a mock salute and said, "Yes, sir."

I came back with the clothes and tossed them through the window to her and said, "Here, it's better than nothing."

As she slipped the old flannel shirt on, she said, "Wow, this is nice and warm."

I said, "Now the jeans, please."

She slipped them on, and said, "They're a little short."

I said, "Well, I don't have legs all the way up to my shoulders, either."

She grinned and said, "Was that a compliment?"

I said, "Just put them on."

#

A few minutes later, she was directing me to her home address about a block away.

As we pulled up to a small duplex that had seen it's better days, I could see a Hello Kitty toy hanging from one of the door knockers, and knew which apartment was hers.

As I shut off the engine, she said, "You know I don't have any money on me, right?"

I said, "No shit."

She said, "I can go inside and get it."

Considering how her night had been already, I said, "Don't worry about it, kid."

She said, "Well, what about your clothes?"

I said, "Keep them. I have more."

As she climbed out of the back seat, she said, "By the way, my name is Sherry."

I said, "Milo. Pleased to have made your

acquaintance."

Standing outside my window now, she said, "Well, Milo, it was fun."

Mulling it over for a few seconds, I said, "Yeah, it was fun, wasn't it?"

With that, she leaned in, kissed me on the cheek, and toddled off toward her front door. When she reached the door, she turned around and said, "Don't be a stranger, Milo."

Then she was gone.

Then so was I.

#

When I got home, it was the same old thing.

Sitting at the kitchen table, counting my nightly fares, which that night wasn't much.

Having a cold beer with a whiskey chaser.

Then a TV dinner and some TV.

Then a long hot shower, to wash all of the scum from the world out there off of me, then to bed.

Then, up the next day about an hour before dusk, to start all over again.

My golden years.

#

I couldn't get my mind off of Sherry that night.

Business had picked up from the night before, five fares in less than an hour, but, otherwise, mostly uneventful.

No punks being dropped off at the jail, no old ladies needing a ride home, or any young, naked ladies running around trying to flag me down.

I had begun to feel cheated.

Then, right out of the blue, came salvation.

I was driving into the North end again, killing some time and trying to cure boredom, when I rounded the corner of New Albany and Jefferson to see an old friend of mine, black guy Willie, walking along, holding a paper sack, no doubt containing a bottle of some cheap, low grade wine.

Willie was an Army veteran who'd come back from the Gulf war a little worse for wear, and instead of coming home to a ticker tape parade in honor of a war hero with a Purple Heart, he ended up living on the streets begging for chump change.

Seeing that he was already hitting the kooky juice early, I thought I had better strike up a conversation now than later.

As I pulled up next to him, I rolled down my window and said, "Well, Willie. What's on the menu tonight? Night Train? Thunderbird?"

He cracked a gap toothed grin and said, "Believe it or not, I'm drinking a nice red wine this evening."

I said, jokingly, "Let me guess; they had a sale at the package store?"

He said, "Yep. Dollar ninety-nine a quart."

I said, "As usual, only the best for my man Willie."

He said, "Yep."

I said, "So, Willie. Have you seen or heard anything interesting out here tonight? I'm getting bored."

He said, "Not really. Why do you think I'm getting drunk this early?"

I knew the feeling. I said, "Well, have a good one, Willie. I'm outa here."

Willie waved at me and said, "Peace out, brother."

I did the same, and drove on into the night.

#

As I drove around the North end aimlessly, the boredom really kicking in by that time, I had decided to drop by the tavern for a cold beer.

I was my own boss, so why not? I couldn't get fired for drinking on the job. Just as long as I knew where to draw the line, I wouldn't get pulled over for drinking and driving, either.

As I pulled into the parking lot, I could see the place was packed, and loud music was blaring from the jukebox inside, so I just passed on by. Call me old school, but my idea of relaxation had little to do with sitting in a bar full of loud, drunken rednecks listening to music that would make most guys my age want to jump out of a moving car.

So, I drove on.

But not far.

#

As I drove on past the tavern, I looked up to see a tall, stocky, African American guy with dreads like Bob Marley standing on the corner waving me down.

He was wearing a North end pimp suit – a silk sweat suit outfit and Nike tennis shoes, but the thing that stood out about him the most was the dried blood on the knuckles of both hands.

But, considering I needed the money, I decided to give him a ride. Besides, I had my trusty .38 revolver loaded with hollow point slugs, so I wasn't worried too much.

I pulled over, rolled down my window, and said, "Need a ride, hoss?"

He immediately began to climb into the front seat, but I said, "Uh uh. Fares are back seat only."

After he'd climbed into the back seat, he lit a cigarette and said, "Just drive, old dude."

I said, "Where to?"

He dug into his pocket, fished out a couple of twenties, and tossed them over the front seat. He said, "Just *drive*, okay?"

I said, "Okay boss."

As we drove along, not going anywhere in particular, I said, "You know, if we're gonna just drive around, I'll need another small deposit."

He dug around in his pocket again, he dug out another twenty, tossed it over the seat, and said, "*Now* can we go, old dude?"

I said, "Sure. By the way, what happened to your hands? Get into a fight with one of your ladies?"

He said, "That's real funny, old school. You should be a comedian."

I said, "Just making an observation, that's all."

He said, "Well, why don't you mind your own business, and we'll get along just fine."

I said, "Well, considering the fact you are in my cab, with blood all over your hands, I have the right to ask you anything I want, Snoop Dog."

He lit a cigarette, and said, "Real funny, you old cracker ass. Best watch your mouth."

I said, "I could say the same for you, snoopy."

He leaned back in the seat, grinned, exposing gold grill work, and said, "You're really funny, you old honky, cracker ass bitch. But you might not feel so funny missing some of your teeth."

I said, "Was that a threat?"

He said, grinning, "Are you a honky bitch?"

That was all it took.

I fished the .38 out of my waistband, cocked the hammer back, and slammed on the brakes. His head hit the back of the front seat, hard, disorienting him momentarily.

I swung around in my seat, pointed the gun right at his face, and said, "You were saying, snoopy?"

Beads of sweat were breaking out on his forehead as he said, "You ain't got the balls, cracker ass."

I said, "That's where you're dead *wrong*, my friend. I tend to shoot women beaters just for the sport of it."

He said, "Bullshit."

I pointed the .38 at his left leg, and said, "Which will it be? Left kneecap, or right? Wait...I got it. How about a hollow point slug to the nuts?"

Raising his bloody hands in submission, he said, "Okay, old school! Just chill!"

I said, "My chill factor begins at twenty bucks per chill."

He fished out several more bills, tossed them over the seat, and said, "Now, let me out, you crazy old cracker."

I said, "The door is unlocked, genius. Let yourself out."

He climbed out, taking off in a dead run as soon

as his Nikes hit the pavement. I pocketed the cash, cracked a big grin, and drove off into the night.

#

I'm not prejudice, mind you.

I just hate any man who beats on a woman. I don't care if your skin is black, white, red, yellow, or even purple with big green polka dots. If you beat on a woman, especially in my presence, I won't hesitate to put a bullet in you.

Just saying.

#

As I drove on into the darkness, my mind kept drifting back to Sherry again.

Not her nudity, mind you. It was thinking about a beautiful young girl, out after dark, buck naked, where some freak could snatch her up and do unspeakable things to her, and dump her in a ditch somewhere.

The very thought of it sent shivers down my spine.

Glancing at my wristwatch, I could see that it wasn't that late yet, so I had decided to drop by and check up on her.

#

When I pulled up to the duplex, her lights weren't on, but I could see the glow of her TV set through the window, so I took a chance and stopped by.

I banged the Hello Kitty door knocker and stood

back, feeling sort of nervous.

A few seconds later, the door opened, and there she stood, dressed in a pair of Hello Kitty Pjs, and cradling a fluffy, tabby striped cat in her arms.

Upon seeing me, her face lit up, amd she said, "Cool! You didn't forget me after all."

I said, "Well, you told me not to be a stranger. Besides, how could I forget *you*?"

Her face flushed as red as her hair as she said, "Yeah, I know."

I said, "Oh no. I didn't mean it *that* way."

She smiled and said, "It's okay, Milo. I know you were embarrassed, too."

I said, "Well, are going to invite me in?"

Sherry said, "Oh, yeah. I'm sorry, come on in."

Her duplex was small, one of those long, shotgun deals, but she had it fixed up real comfy and cozy.

And everywhere, kitty stuff.

Kitty curtains, kitty throw pillows, kitty couch cover. One thing was for sure, she loved cats.

As we sat down at her tiny kitchen table, she said, "Want something to drink? I have coffee, orange juice, or beer."

I said, "Beer sounds good."

She placed her kitty on the floor next to her food bowl, grabbed me a beer from the fridge, and handed it to me. I said, "You're not joining me?"

She said, "I think I have had enough alcohol for now, don't you?"

I couldn't help but grin as I said, "I see your point."

She said, "So, to what do I owe this special visit?"

I sipped my beer and said, "No special reason, I

just wanted to see if you were okay."

She smiled and said, "My Knight in shining armor. Or could it be my guardian angel?"

I said, "I'd like to think it was the latter."

She said, "Me, too."

Glancing around, I said, "I see you really like kitty cats."

She said, "I *love* kitty cats."

I said, "They can be theraputic."

She said, "Ah...so you didn't have much of a father figure either, huh?"

I said, "In my so called family, it was my mother who was the absentee parent."

She said, "Either way, it's good to have a substitute when you need one. What was yours?"

I said, "Alcohol, straight up. And cigarettes."

She said, "Whatever floats your boat, I always say."

Sipping my beer, I said, "I must agree."

She said, "So, how's business tonight?"

I said, "Kinda boring, actually. That is, until I met up with Snoop Dog."

Seeeming confused, she said, "Come again?"

I said, "Never mind."

There was an uncomfortable silence between us for a few moments, then she said, "You know, if you're bored with me, you can leave."

I said, "Oh no, it's not that."

She said, "What is it, then? I mean, I think we have things in common."

I said, "It's not you, really. And I agree, we do have things in common, although it might be the *wrong* things."

She said, "What do you mean?"

I said, "You know, depressing things."

She just said, "Oh."

I said, "It's not you, really."

She said, "I hope not, because I *like* you."

I said, "The feeling is mutual."

She said, "Well, that's a good thing."

I said, "I hope so."

I drained the rest of my beer and just sat here like a statue, looking at her. She said, "Penny for your thoughts?"

I lit a cigarette and said, "I was just thinking about how lucky I was to meet you."

She smiled and said, "Well, I was lucky too, remember?"

I said, "Yes, I'll never forget. Well, I best get going, I have more money to make tonight."

She said, "I can understand that. Why don't you stop by after work? I can't sleep for some reason, and I could use the company."

Standing to leave, I said, "It's a date."

She said, jokingly, "That sounds interesting."

Turning to leave, I said, "Behave yourself."

#

As I pulled away from her duplex, it suddenly hit me that I had to pick up Billy at the county jail in the morning, which would make me late for my date.

But I *did* need the extra cash. What I'd acquired from snoopy would be gone as soon as I hit the grocery store and filled up my tank.

So, onward I went into the night.

#

I had two more fares before I picked Billy up.

A lady from a bar who was too drunk to open the back door, and her boyfriend, whom, judging by his taste in clothing, had forgotten that disco music had died a long time ago.

Then, according to my wristwatch, it was time to pick Billy up at the county jail.

As I pulled up to the back door of the jail, there was Billy, sitting on an old milk crate and puffing on a cigarette nervously. His hands were obviously shaking, so I knew he'd had a bad weekend in jail.

As he climbed in the back seat, I could see in my rear view mirror that he'd been beat up. His right eye was almost swelled shut, and his lower lip was busted and caked with dried blood.

I said, "Damn, Billy boy. What the hell happened to you?"

He just said, "I'd rather not talk about it."

Leaning over the seat, I said, "I bet. But, remember who you're talking to here. You know you can tell me anything."

He said, "Promise you won't say nothing to anybody?"

I said, "You know me better than that."

He said, "Just drive."

As we pulled away from the jail, he said, "It was some big ugly fucker named Gibby Fox."

I said, "You mean Gilbert Fox?"

He said, "Yeah, that's him."

Gilbert "Gibby" Fox was *really* crazy.

Local legend {or gossip, most likely} has it that his parents were crazy too, and were alcoholics, and his mama even sniffed airplane glue while she was pregnant with Gibby.

But that was just the *beginning* of Gibby's pathetic life at the hands of two homicidal maniacs.

It was also rumored that when Gibby was just a toddler, he was playing with a set of toy soldiers his grandmother had given him for Christmas, his father walked in to see the living room floor strewn with toys and candy wrappers, and had gone into a fit of rage that left Gibby with a broken arm, a skull fracture, two missing teeth, and a black eye.

He barely survived that incident – and more bizarre incidents were yet to come.

As he grew older {and crazier} he had carried on the family tradition by becoming a problem drinker and drug addict with an extremely volatile temper.

Tonight, he had taken out his frustrations on Billy boy.

I said, "Why did he hit you?"

Billy said, "Since when does Gibby Fox need a *reason* to hit you?"

I said, glumly, "That's true."

Billy said, "I was just sitting in the day room, watching TV, when he walked by, and stomped on my right foot. Said it was in his way. I called him a fat ass retard and he busted my face."

I said, "Where was the day room guard?"

Billy snickered and said, "Where do you think? Sitting inside his little cubby hole, sipping coffee and stuffing his fat face with day old donuts."

I said, "That figures."

Billy said, "Yes it does."

I said, "Did you report it?"

Billy said, "Snitches get stitches, you know that."

I said, "Yes, I do. Sorry, Billy."

He said, "Can we stop talking about it now? I feel like a punk already."

I said, "Done."

#

After dropping Billy off, I was definitely in the mood for another cold beer.

And a shot of whiskey.

Fire water.

Liquid salvation, in the form of the demon alcohol.

Call it whatever you want, I needed some – and fast.

I stopped by Sherry's place.

As I knocked, I was thinking about the fact that I didn't care what happened when she opened that door, as long as it was something *normal*.

Quiet and soothing.

The door opened as my heart felt like it was beating right out of my chest.

There she was, clad in nothing but a tank top t-shirt and thong undies.

She was smiling.

So was I.

As I stepped inside and closed the door behind me, no words were spoken between us.

We just fell into each other's arms and let it

happen.

#

Afterward, as I lay in the dark next to a beautiful angel, I felt no guilt over my actions whatsoever.

There was no reason to feel guilty over just being *human*.

All humans have thoughts and desires and even lust in their hearts, at one time or another.

Where Sherry and I were concerned, I was her guardian angel, and she was my lifeline back to reality.

So, nope, no guilt whatsoever.

As I lay there smoking a cigarette, staring at the ceiling and wishing she would wake up. As though she could read my mind in her sleep, she opened her big green eyes and said, "Morning."

I said, "Morning, sunshine girl."

She smiled and said, "You're silly."

I said, "This is true."

She said, "So, what's on your agenda for today?"

I leaned in closer, kissed her little pouty lips, and said, "What do you think?"

She grinned and said, jokingly, "Hmm...well, do you think you handle another round, old school?"

I said, "Just watch me."

#

Later that morning, as we sat at the kitchen table watching her cat, Floof, playing with a catnip stuffed dill pickle, and sipping some fortified coffee, she said, "So...what should we do with the rest of our day?"

I said, "I was thinking, maybe a picnic?"

Her face lit up as she said, "That sounds great. I haven't been on a picnic since I was a kid."

I said, "Me neither," and was being honest. My so called parent's idea of a picnic had been sitting on the front porch eating fried bologna sandwiches.

She said, "And for our choice of picnic food?"

I said, "Why not be traditional, and pick up some lunchmeat, hoagie buns, and chips?"

She said, "Cool. Can we have dill pickles too?"

I said, "Why of course. Anything for my Queen."

She blushed and said, "You think I'm a Queen?"

I said, "You're *my* little Queen, yes."

She stood up, sat on my lap, gave me a big juicy kiss, and said, "Then that makes you my *King*."

I said, "Yes, it does. And remember, my Queen has to do *anything* her King asks her to do."

She said, "This is going to be a *very* interesting relationship."

Giving her a big hug, I said, "I sure hope so."

#

We had a real nice little picnic at a local park, and even brought Floof the cat along to keep us entertained.

Afterward, we went back to her place for a well deserved nap before I started another shift. I was going to take the night off, but I wanted to check on Billy boy.

I had done several brief stints in the local jail

when I was much younger, but I did remember how intimidating some of the other inmates could be.

After a hot shower I had kissed my Queen goodbye for the moment and drove over to Billy's place around dusk.

As I came to the intersection close to his building, I could see flashing lights and hear loud voices echoing off of the nearby homes.

As I turned the corner I could see two police cars with their lights flashing, as well as an EMT vehicle parked nearby.

As well as a coroner's van.

As I slowly drove closer to the scene, I could see one of our local Detectives, Harlan Crow, talking to one of the officers. I pulled up a little closer, rolled down my window, and waved at him to get his attention.

He walked over to me with a solemn look on his face and said, "If you're here to pick up Billy, you're a little too late, Milo."

Feeling my guts tighten up, I said, "I just dropped him off day before yesterday."

Crow said, "After which he apparently hung himself in the shower. With an electric cord. His neighbor found him today when she dropped by to see if she could use his phone."

My heart sank in my chest. I said, "He had told me about Gibby Fox busting his face."

Crow said, "Yeah, I saw his face. You know how it is, Milo. Some guys can take it, some can't take it."

I said, "Yeah. Why don't you put that on his gravestone? It would make a wonderful epitaph."

Crow said, "I'm sorry, Milo. I really am."

"Not as sorry as I am, I bet," I said, and pulled

away.

#

I just drove around for a while, not really going anywhere in particular, just driving and watching the darkness go by like a blur.

My whole *mind* was a blur.

I needed a drink.

#

I dropped by the local package store around eight pm, grabbed me a bottle of single malt scotch and some smokes. I figured if I was gonna get as drunk as a barrel full of retarded monkeys, I might as well drink the good stuff.

I took a drive to the river bottoms, where I used to go fishing as a kid, and just sat there watching the moon glitter like a big diamond on the surface of the murky water, my mind racing with ghastly visions of Billy's last moments on Earth.

With each cruel, twisting yank of the cord against his flesh, I took another drink.

I woke up laying on the ground, hours later, the full moon looming over me like a big white skull.

After so long, I staggered to my feet and drove over to Sherry's place.

#

To my surprise, her lights were still on.

No doubt in anticipation of her King dropping by for a visit.

Before I even had a chance to knock on the door, she was already standing there, clad in her Hello Kitty pajamas.

She said, "You don't look so good."

I said, "I don't feel so good, either."

She said, "What happened?"

I said, "A friend of mine died. Well, he killed himself, that is."

She reached out and hugged me tight, and I began crying like a baby.

#

Later, as we sat at the kitchen table sipping black coffee, she said, "So, what was your friend like?"

Lighting a cigarette, I said, "He was okay, I guess."

She said, "He must have been okay, for you to be so upset."

I said, "He was just a young fella who made some bad choices, and paid for it. He didn't deserve to be so sad and hopeless."

She said, "I'm so sorry, Milo. Is there anything I can do to help?"

I sipped my coffee and said, "You already have, just being here for me."

She stood up and sat on my lap, kissed me on the cheek, and said, "I know the feeling."

Wanting to change the subject, I said, "So, how about a nap and some dinner? I'll make you some of my famous bourbon cheeseburgers."

She said, "I never had a burger made with bourbon before. Sounds interesting."

I said, "It's all in the secret recipe."

She said, "Sounds like a plan. Last one in the bed is a rotten egg."

She beat me to the bed, of course, me being the rotten egg that I am.

#

I felt a little better after a nap and a shower, but not much.

I didn't tell her that, though. I wanted my Sherry to enjoy herself and shine like the Queen she was.

Her presence was the only thing that saved my soul that night.

Although the bourbon burgers weren't too bad, either.

Or my dessert.

#

After dessert, we took another nap, this time a much longer nap, catching up on sleep and snuggling like two cozy kittens.

I felt like a kid again; a bad case of puppy love, infatuation, my mother would have called it, but I didn't care. I was happy for the first time in years, and nothing was going to screw it up for me.

That is, unless, she got tired of me.

One thing was for sure, I wasn't going to get tired of her anytime soon.

#

After the usual late afternoon kisses and a long hot shower, I was on the road again around dusk.

I was driving down Second Street, on my way North, when I was flagged down by my old buddy, Willie.

As I pulled over to the curb, I didn't even get a chance to say hello before he began ranting. He said, "Have you heard?"

I said, "About Billy boy? Yeah, I heard."

Willie said, "No, about Gibby Fox."

He had my full attention then. I said, "What about the big fat ugly psycho?"

He said, "He's out of jail already. He's been sitting at the bar, bragging about how he stomped Billy's ass."

I could already feel the anger boiling inside of me as I said, "Oh, is that so?"

He said, "Yep. That ornery asshole is drunk as hell and talking all sorts of bullshit."

I said, "Yeah, well, he won't be for long."

I pulled away before Willie could comment any further.

#

I sat across the street from the bar, in the dark, my .38 ready and loaded for bear.

As I sat there, I could just imagine Gibby sitting at the bar, regaling his fellow drunks with tales of being a bad ass and how many asses he's kicked while he was in lockup.

Yeah buddy! I spent my time in lockup kicking ass and taking no prisoners! Little faggot bitches!

The thought made me want to climb out of my taxi, walk into the bar, and blow his brains out.

But, considering the fact that most guys my age were a target in lockup too, I had opted for a different way to handle things. Besides, I'd never see my Queen again, and I couldn't bear that thought.

So, I sipped beer, chain smoked, and waited for Gibby to leave the bar.

#

I didn't have to wait too long.

Within the next thirty minutes or so, here came Gibby, most likely out of money and in a surly mood, wanting to kick the ass of some other poor soul who just happens to be a lot smaller and weaker than him.

As he staggered out the front door of the bar, he glanced my way, and waved me over.

My plan was working out perfectly.

I pulled a u-turn and pulled up right beside him, rolled down my window, and said, "Need a ride, hoss?"

Always the smartass prick, Gibby said, "No, dumbass. I just flagged you down for the hell of it."

I said, "No need to get nasty, my chubby friend. Where to?"

He climbed into the back seat, he said, "Just drive and I'll tell you when to stop."

I said, "You got it."

Then off we went into the darkness.

After several minutes of listening to Gibby burp, fart, and curse under his breath, I'd had enough.

I pulled over next to an empty parking lot, slammed on the brakes, pulled out the .38, and leaned over the seat, pointing it right at his big fat face, and said, "Ride is over."

He looked stunned at first, then gathered his wits about him enough to say, ""Are you crazy, you old fart?"

I said, "Far from it, my fat, smelly friend."

He cleared his throat and said, "You better be willing to pull that trigger, you point it at Gibby Fox."

I laughed and said, "Oh yes, I know. Mr Billy bad ass. I should be shaking in my boots. You beat up any little kids today, or kick any puppies?"

He said, "Screw you, you old shit. I don't have to kick ass on any kids. I'd rather kick *your* ass."

I cocked the hammer back on the .38, and said, "Just like you beat Billy's ass in lockup? I don't think so, you asshole."

His chest swelling in defiance, he said, "Who do you think you're talking to, you old fart?"

I said, "I think I'm talking to a piece of shit, but that's just my opinion."

He said, "Billy was a little punk, just like you. How about I take that gun, and shove it up your ass? How's that?"

I said, "That sounds like a threat to me. I better defend myself."

Then I aimed the gun at Gibby's right kneecap,

and pulled the trigger.

He began howling like a wounded animal, squirming around in the back seat, as I pulled out my phone and dialed 911.

Then I grabbed a large hunting knife from my glovebox, and tossed it into the back seat. The idiot actually picked it up – and getting his fingerprints on the handle in the process – and screamed, "Stay away from me old man, or I'll cut you good!"

My plan had worked out perfectly.

#

By the time the police, the EMTs, and Crow had showed up, Gibby was nothing more than a big fat smelly blubbering mess squirming around on the back floorboard, holding his ruined kneecap amd balling like a baby with a dirty diaper.

As the EMTs loaded Gibby into the back of an ambulance, Crow was glaring at me and said, "Really, Milo? You shot the poor bastard in the kneecap?"

I said, "He wasn't worth going to prison, so I opted for a more appropriate reaction."

Crow said, "You are a very *lucky* man, Milo. If he hadn't had that knife in his hand, I'd be arresting you for assault with a deadly weapon."

I said, "Yeah, I was *very* lucky."

Crow said, "Uh huh. Well, I think we're done here for now. Do you think you can finish your shift tonight without killing anyone?"

I said, "Sure. I think the public is safe."

Walking away, Crow said, "It wasn't the public I was worried about."

                            #

I drove around the North end for a while, sipping a half pint and chain smoking until my nerves were a bit more steady, then I went back home to my cramped little apartment and drank some more.

By the time I was too drunk to drive, it was too late to drop by Sherry's place.

So I took a nap.

                            #

A few hours and several nightmares later, I woke up to the sound of someone rapping on my door.

It was Sherry.

As I stood there in the doorway, in my boxer shorts and a t-shirt, feeling like an elephant had stomped on my head, she said, jokingly, "Love your outfit."

I said, "I thought I'd go with my sexy look today. Is it working?"

She said, "Believe it or not, I do feel a stirring in my loins."

I said, "You're weird."

She smiled and said, "But you love me."

I said, "Before we discuss our love life, may we please step inside? I'm kinda shy about my gorgeous body."

She stepped past me, saying, "Yeah, right."

We sat at the kitchen table sipping fortified coffee and having a smoke when she said, "You seem nervous."

I said, "Didn't have a very good night."

She said, "Yes, I heard."

I said, "Come again?"

She said, "It's all over social media, how you shot some guy trying to rob you."

I said, "Ah, yes, the world wide web."

She said, "I'm surprised you didn't drop by my place after it was over. I was worried."

I said, "I'm sorry, babe. I was just so damn tired is all. I'm better now."

She said, "You don't look better."

I said, "Wow, thanks a lot."

She sat on my lap, kissed me on the cheek, and said, "I didn't mean it that way."

I said, "I know."

She kissed me on the lips the second time, and said, "Wanna take another nap? I could use one too."

Yawning, my head still pounding, I said, "I think that's a wonderful idea."

#

We slept for almost seven hours.

It was past my regular shift time by then, so I didn't even concern myself with driving my cab.

Instead, Sherry and I just hung around my place for a while, playing cards and having a drink or two and then a mild dinner of leftover chili.

By then, she said she needed to go check on Floof, give her some fresh food and water, and I said I'd go along. I knew it was in my best interest not to be alone at that point in time, and clear my head.

But each time I even blinked my eyes, let alone close them, I saw images of Billy boy hanging from his shower rod.

Yeah...I needed a break.

I needed my Queen.

#

After giving Floof some fresh food and water, we sat down at the table for a game of cards.

Strip poker, that is.

I kept losing, and was I sure she was stacking the deck.

By the time I was down to my boxers and socks, I said, "You're cheating."

With a mischievous little grin, she said, "Come again?"

I said, "You're stacking the deck."

She said, "You're just a sore loser."

Before I had a chance to retort, my phone rang. The screen told me it was Crow. I sighed and said, "Excuse me dear. I better get this."

I answered and said, "Yeah?"

Crow said, "Just thought I'd let you know, Gibby Fox intends to sue you for his hospital bill."

I said, "Oh yeah? Well, he can kiss my ass."

Crow said, "No, you can kiss *his* ass. He has a right to sue you under the law."

I said, "Then the law can kiss my ass."

Crow said, "Wrong again. Since you have declined to press charges, all we can do is fine him, slap him on his grimy little hand, and set him loose."

I said, "Well, then *all* of you can kiss my ass."

I hung up.

Sherry said, "Problem?"

I said, "The asshole I shot wants to sue me."

She said, "I thought it was self defense."

I said, "It was."

She said, "Well, that sucks."

I sipped my drink and said, "Yes, it does. But, let's get back to our game for now, shall we?"

She said, "You're going to lose."

I said, "I don't care."

#

After I'd lost my boxers, I gave up.

For the rest of the morning, we just sat around and listened to the radio and drank beer and played kissy face. I was feeling like a kid again.

But mostly just acting like one.

I stopped drinking by mid afternoon, knowing I would be driving later, and Sherry hit the couch for a nap with Floof.

I didn't bother waking her up as I left, she needed the rest.

#

Right past dusk, I was cruising the North end, watching the usual spots; bars, street corners, restaurants, the hospital parking lot.

By right past midnight I'd had only two fares, one an old lady at the local Dollar General store, and Willie, whom I'd found sound asleep on the sidewalk.

After dropping him off, I'd driven back by Sherry's place to see her TV light on, and, figuring she was still taking a nap, just drove on past for the time being.

I drove on South then, to see if the normal part of town might be in need of my services.

No luck.

It was like after the incident with Gibby, folks were afraid of riding in my taxi. Like it was cursed now, or some such nonsense.

Which brought to mind maybe I better take it to a car wash facility and clean the back floorboard.

When I arrived at the car wash, luckily for me, there were no other customers, so I had the place to myself.

The blood stain on the floorboard was very visible to the naked eye, and knowing that wouldn't exactly boost business, I proceeded to do my best to clean it up.

After so much time had gone by, I'd realized that nothing the carwash machine had in stock was going to get rid of the blood stain, I'd opted to use my box cutter to completely remove that section of carpeting, and toss it in the dumpster.

The bare floorboard wasn't all that attractive either, but it was better than blood stains and tiny pieces of Gibby's kneecap.

By the time I was done, I was ready for a cold beer break. But realizing that the local package stores were closed by then, I ended up driving by my place to grab a couple of beers from the icebox.

When I climbed back into the driver's seat, my dashboard clock informed me that it was only two and half hours to daylight. So I climbed out of the driver's seat, took a seat on the front porch, and drank my beer.

By the time I'd finished my third beer, I was sound asleep.

#

I drove back to Sherry's place around nine am.

When I pulled up, she was outside, wearing a two piece bathing suit, watering her small flower garden. I couldn't help but think how even flowers paled in comparison to her own beauty.

When she saw me, she gave me a big wave and a smile, and I could feel my heart beating a little bit faster again.

I was *hooked.*

She said, "Breakfast is ready."

As I approached the garden, I said, "You shouldn't have."

She said, "Well, a working man can't live on beer alone."

I said, "True. He needs good kisses too."

She threw her arms around me and kissed me and that's the last thing I remember until I sat down to eat.

#

As we sat at the table eating Cheerios, Floof rubbed against my leg and purred. I said, "I think I have a new fan."

Sherry said, "Cats are very intelligent, actually. She is simply showing her good taste in men."

I looked down at Floof and said, "Good kitty."

Sherry said, "So, how was last night?"

I said, "Not so good, to be honest."

She said, "Aw...I'm sorry."

I said, "It's no big deal. I have busy nights and slow ones. It comes with the territory."

She said, "It must get lonely."

I said, "More boring than lonely."

She said, jokingly, "Wow, thanks a lot."

I said, "You know what I mean."

She said, "You know, I have an idea."

I said, "Is that good or bad?"

She said, "Smartass."

I said, "Go on, I'm listening."

She said, "I get really bored around here too. Why don't I ride along with you in your cab sometimes? I think it would be fun."

After mulling it over for a few moments, I said, "You know, I bet it would be fun."

She said, "How about tonight?"

I said, "Why not? It's a date."

She said, "Milo, I have to admit something."

I said, "Oh no. Let me guess; you used to be a man, right?"

She said, "No, silly boy. But I'm living on unemployment checks right now, and I don't have much to offer a man."

I said, "So? I live on a military pension and cab fare. What's the big deal?"

She said, "I just wanted to be honest with you about *everything*, that's all."

I said, "Well, you've been honest, and so have I. Now let's move on."

She cracked a smile and said, "Yes, sir."

I said, "Don't call me sir, it make me feel old."

She said with a grin, "You *are* old."

I said, "I'm only seventeen years older than you,

Miss smarty pants."

She said, "I was just kidding."

I said, "I know, sugar pop."

She said, "Sugar pop?"

I said, "It's my new nickname for you. Do you like it?"

Flashing me a playful wink, she said, "Yes, I do, very much. I have one for you too."

I said, "Which is?"

She said, "Stud puppy. You like it?"

I said, "Works for me."

She said, "I bet it does, my stud puppy."

I said, "Speaking of which, how about a little "nap" before our little adventure tonight?"

She said, "Sounds great."

#

And it was.

After another long hot shower, we were on the road.

As we approached the North end of town, we passed by the bar where Sherry had seeked a ride that fateful night, and I couldn't resist teasing her a little bit.

As we passed by, I said, "I bet that place brings back fond memories for you."

She said, "Not really, Mr smartass."

I said, "Are you sure? They might be looking for a dancer."

She said, glumly, "I was drunk and stupid and desperate, and I'd rather not talk about it."

I said, "Sorry."

She said, "I know."

We had just finished passing by the bar when I spotted Willie strolling down the street carrying a brown paper bag, no doubt containing the most recent red tag sale wine from the package store. I said, "There's a friend of mine. Wanna meet him?"

Sherry took a glance out the window and said, "Sure, I guess so. If he is a friend of yours, he's a friend of mine too."

As Willie approached the corner, I pulled over and rolled down my window and said, "How's it hanging, old friend?"

Wille stopped and said, "A little to the left. And yourself?"

I said, "Just trying to make a few bucks, as usual."

Willie said, "Good luck."

I said, "This is Sherry, my new lady."

Willie leaned in closer, and gawking at her long legs, said, "Well, the pleasure is all *mine*."

Sherry blushed and said, "Thank you, Willie."

I said, "Down boy, be a good boy."

Willie said, "You better be more concerned with the bad boys who are looking for you."

I said, "Come again?"

Willie said, "Gibby Fox is still in the hospital, but he's been relaying messages to his beer buddies and his relatives out here. He's looking for some payback."

I said, "Yeah, well, like I told Crow, Gibby can kiss my ass."

Willie said, "He doesn't want to kiss your ass, he wants to *shoot* your ass."

I said, "Well, screw him and his buddies. And his relatives most likely aren't even smart enough to load a gun, let alone fire one."

Willie said, "I'm just giving you fair warning, brother. I know you don't rightly give a damn."

I said, "That's right, I don't. But thanks for the heads-up, anyway."

Willie said, "My pleasure. So, what you are two lovebirds up to this evening?"

Sherry said, "We're going to make some money, then we're going back to my place and have sex."

Willie said, "Sounds like a good plan."

I said, "Oh, believe me, it is."

Willie said, "Well, I better get moving. I have a few more blocks to go."

I said, "Need a ride?"

He said, "Thanks, but I'd rather hoof it tonight, I need the exercise."

I said, "You and me both."

Then Willie was on his way, and so were Sherry and I.

#

About an hour later, I still hadn't had any fares, and to be honest, was losing the gumption to keep trying.

As we pulled up to a corner market to buy some cigarettes, Sherry said, "It's okay if you want to give up for tonight, Milo. I'm getting kind of bored myself, too."

I said, "I'm sorry, babe. I thought we'd have more fun than this."

She leaned over and kissed me on the cheek, and said, "Just grab our cigarettes and we'll go home."

I said, "I don't give up that easily, you know that."

She said, "Milo, not to upset you, but did you ever stop to think that maybe people are *afraid* to ride in your cab now, because of you shooting Gibby in the back seat?"

I said, glumly, "Yes, I've already thought about it, and maybe you're right. I just hate to admit that I'm defeated."

She said, "You're still *my* hero."

I said, "And you're still my Queen."

She said, "Let's go back to my place, my hero."

I said, "Sounds good to me."

#

We spent the rest of the evening playing cards and sipping cold beer.

But no strip poker; I had realized that I wasn't a very good loser.

Instead, Sherry had introduced me to a card game called Uno. It was sort of a weird game, but I caught on pretty quick.

But it wasn't as *fun* as strip poker.

#

By around one am, we were both pretty worn out, so we'd decided to make it an early night for a change.

But I couldn't sleep.

I kept thinking about what Willie had told me, about Gibby and his buddies wanting some payback, but I didn't want Sherry to know I was concerned with it. She didn't have anything to do with it, and I wanted to keep it that way.

But how long could I keep *her* safe?

Sleep never came.

#

The next morning, Sherry was up early.

Upon seeing me lying there with my bleary eyes wide open, she said, "Bad night, I presume?"

I said, "Don't ask."

She said, "I'm sorry."

I said, "It's not you, it's me."

She said, "That sounds like a lame excuse for a breakup."

I said, "Sorry. But, I couldn't sleep last night thinking about your safety."

She said, "If you're referring to Gibby and his asshole friends, I can take care of myself."

I said, "Of that I have no doubt. Still, I want you safe at *all* times."

She said, "I don't need a babysitter."

I said, "I won't be your babysitter, I'll be your bodyguard."

She said, "Just what are you proposing?"

I said, "That you live with me for now, you and Miss Floof, of course."

She said, "So, in other words, I have to rearrange my whole life because of this asshole?"

I said, "I'm sorry you feel that way, but it's going to be temporary."

She sat there fuming over my idea for a few moments, took a deep breath, and said, "Well, okay. But you need to do something about this asshole soon."

I said, "Oh, don't worry, I intend to."

#

Sherry had packed only the essentials – clothes, personal items, and Floof of course – and by the time she'd unpacked it all at my place, she looked to be completely worn out physically, and mentally.

By the time we sat down at my kitchen table for a cold beer, she said, "I hope we can have a nice, relaxing, peaceful evening."

Before I could say a word, my phone rang. I looked at the screen to see it was Crow again.

Sherry giggled as I rolled my eyes and answered the phone. I said, "Yes, Mr Crow? What can I do for you?"

Crow said, "It's what I can do for you."

I said, "Let me guess; Gibby's Uncle is going to drop an atomic bomb on my apartment, right?"

Crow said, "Not quite that severe, but close. He is throwing another pissy fit at the hospital, saying that you *framed* him."

I said, "Framed him? How so?"

Crow said, "He says you placed that knife close to him after you shot him, so you could claim self defense."

I said, "That's bullshit, Crow. You know what a crazy, lying sack of shit he is."

Crow said, "Of course I do. But under the law, I felt I had to relay the message."

I said, "Well, you've done your civic duty. Is there anything else unpleasant you need to tell me?"

Crow said, "Nope, I think that about covers it for

now."

I hung up.

Sherry said, "So, I gather Gibby has found another way to screw with you?"

I said, glumly, "Yep."

She said, "So, what are you going to do?"

I said, "*Nothing*, that's what. You and me are going to sit here and have a good time and not worry about anything but *having* a good time."

Her face lit up and she said, "Now, that's what I needed to hear. What shall we do first, my stud puppy?"

I said, "Is there anything such as strip Uno?"

She grinned and said, "I don't see why not."

#

I wasn't any better at strip Uno than I was at strip poker.

By the time I was down to my undies, I said, "How about we order a pizza?"

She giggled and said, "You're just trying to avoid the inevitable, and you know it."

I said, "Guilty as charged."

She said, "But a pizza does sound good."

I said, "See? So, what flavor do we want?"

She said, "How about the good old, all American, cheese pizza, with extra cheese?"

I said, "And for me, a laxative for dessert."

She flashed me a playful wink and said, "I already have dessert covered, remember?"

I said, "How about we have our dessert first, and pizza later?"

She said, "My thoughts exactly."

#

After we had our dessert, we ordered the pizza – and I still needed a laxative.

But inbetween, we had a lot of fun, and it was one of the best nights we'd shared together. One of those nights that you hoped would last forever.

But as usual, sleep eventually caught up to us, and we slept for hours, and I didn't even worry about going to work, and driving around all night for nothing.

The way I looked at it, Gibby might have done me a favor that night, making me realize there was something more important to do with my life other than drive a cab ten hours a night for nothing, just picking up assholes, when I had something much more important waiting for me at home.

But I still hated his guts.

#

The next day, though, our blessed, blissful silence was interrupted once again with bad news.

Crow had called me at th crack of dawn, the tone of his voice very nervous as he said, "I just wanted you to know, Gibby was released early this morning."

I said, "And let me guess; under the law, you couldn't do anything about it, right?"

Crow said, "What do you want me to do, Milo? Shoot him?"

I said, "That would be a good start."

Crow said, "Well, at least I did give you fair

warning."

I said, "Yes, you did."

Then I hung up.

Sherry rolled over and said, "Now what?"

I said, "Gibby was released this morning."

She yawned and said, "So what?"

I said, "So, nothing. Crow was just giving me the obligatory heads-up."

She said, "Okay, you've been warned. Let's go back to sleep."

Which is what we did – that is, until we had a very rude and loud awakening.

#

It happened around ten am.

We had been a deep, peaceful sleep, when we both sat bolt upright in bed, at the loud, terrifiying sound of my front window being shattered.

Sherry was crying and freaking out as I jumped out of bed, slipped my jeans on, and ran into the living room to see a chunk of concrete as big as a soccer ball lying in the floor, with a note attached to it.

I leaned down and picked it up, to see the note was written in human blood.

All it said was:

Your next

The stupid assholes couldn't even spell a death threat correctly – and had done this in broad daylight.

I ran into the kitchen, shut off the night light, and

went back to the living room to look out the window.

There was nobody there, on foot or otherwise. Like they were a ghost.

I walked back to the bedroom to find Sherry with her knees pulled up to her chest, and the blanket draped over her, shaking all over, and Floof hiding under the bed.

I said, "It's okay, they're gone now."

She said, "It's okay?!"

I said, "Just calm down, babe. Someone is just trying to scare us."

Lighting a cigarette, she said, "They're doing a good job of it."

I picked up my phone from the night stand and said, "I'm going to call Crow."

She said, "Why? So he can come over and give you more bad news and be a smartass?"

I said, "This is true. But I think he should know about it."

Rolling her eyes, she said, "Fine, call Crow. I'm going to take a shower."

#

Surprisingly, Crow was on the scene within minutes.

As he looked at the mess in the living room floor, he said, "Well, they know how to get their point across."

I said, "No shit. How about the note scrawled in *blood*? Is that just trying to scare us?"

He said, "It's probably pig blood. I wouldn't place much emphasis on that, either."

I said, "I know they're a bunch of retarded hillbillies, but they are *dangerous* hillbillies."

Crow said, "Gibby isn't behind this, he's in no shape to have done it."

I said, "I don't care if it was his grandma, we need some protection here. I'm not only watching my own ass now."

About that time, Sherry came out of the bathroom wearing my nightrobe and said, "That's right, Mr Crow. I'm here now too."

Crow said, "I'm sorry, ma'am. Tell you what I'll do, Milo. I'll place a patrol car out back, and have one drive by on a regular basis. Best I can do."

I said, "Imagine that."

Crow said, "Meaning?"

Sherry cut in and said, "I believe Milo is voicing his opinion about your job performance, or lack thereof."

Crow shot her a dirty look and said, "I do the best I can, ma'am."

I cut in and said, "Just keep an eye on my apartment, Crow. That shouldn't be that difficult for a man of your obvious talents."

Crow said, "Was that an insult?"

I said, "Is Gibby Fox mentally deranged?"

#

After Crow left, Sherry and I cleaned up the broken glass, and I placed a piece of plywood over the busted window until I could get it fixed.

Sitting at the kitchen table afterward, sipping some single malt scotch, Sherry said, "I want an honest answer to an important question."

I sipped my drink and said, "I'll do my best."

She said, "Just *how* crazy is Gibby and his family?"

I said, "As crazy as a pack of drunken, retarded hyenas."

She said, "That's just great."

I said, "You asked."

She said, "I want a gun."

I said, "Fair enough. Are you familiar with the use of firearms?"

She said, "You load it, aim it, and shoot. Right?"

I said, "Well, there's a little more to it than that, but at least you're on the right track."

Sipping her drink, she said, "Then *teach* me."

So I did.

#

That afternoon, we drove out to a secluded spot I used to frequent for target practice, and I taught her the basics.

Treat every gun as if it was already loaded. Always keep the muzzle of the firearm pointed in a safe direction. Always keep your finger off the trigger and outside the trigger guard unless you intend to fire the weapon.

Well, you get the idea.

But Sherry was sort of confused at first.

By the time I'd pointed out all of the gun safety basics, I'd figured she would change her mind.

But not my Queen; oh no, she seemed excited by it all, and couldn't wait to get started.

#

By the time we were done with her first lesson, I was already confident that she was going to be a natural.

But our good day was short lived when we arrived back at my place.

When we pulled up in front of my building, I could see a tall, stocky man wearing dirty work boots, a pair of coveralls, a dirty t-shirt, and a baseball cap on backwards, sitting on the front steps, smoking a cigar and staring at us as we parked the cab.

As I shut off the engine, I handed Sherry the apartment keys and said, "Just go straight into the building and lock the apartment door behind you and wait for me."

She said, "Why? I have the .25 in my purse."

I said, "Please, just humor me, okay?"

She said, "Okay, but I'll be watching through the window."

I said, "Fair enough."

As she walked by the man, he barely even noticed her presence, his eyes fixed on me. As I approached the front steps, he said, "Damn, brother. You're on a bad luck streak, aren't you?"

I said, "Come again?"

He cracked a gap toothed grin and said, "Well, first of all, the Taxi Land cab company seems to be going down the toilet, then somebody busts your window. I'd call that bad luck."

I said, "I'd call it a direct attack on me and my property."

He said, "Call it what you want, but I'd say you brought this bad luck streak on yourself."

I said, "How so?"

Gap tooth said, "Well, you go around shooting folks in the kneecap, and acting like it's just fine and dandy that you did so, you could tend to make an enemy or two."

I stepped closer, and said, "He had it coming. He pulled a knife on me."

Gap tooth said, "That's not the way I heard it."

I said, "I don't rightly give the hairy crack of a rat's ass what you heard, because I know how it went down."

Gap tooth stood up then, towering over me by at least four inches, staring at me menacingly, trying to intimidate me. I just stood my ground, staring right back at him, in his beady little eyes. I said, "It doesn't have to be this way."

Gap tooth said, "Yeah, it sorta does."

I said, "Well, don't say I didn't warn you."

I slowly reached behind my back with my right hand, grasping the .38 in my waistband, and slowly bringing it up where he could see it. He just laughed and said, "What are you going to do with that little gun? Shoot frogs?"

I raised the .38 in thr air, cocked the hammer back, and pointed it at his face, and said, "No, I'm going to shoot you, Jethro, if you don't leave right now."

Gap tooth just stood there staring at me again, and, apparently realizing I wasn't just making an idle threat, backed up a bit and said, "It's okay, little man. But I'll be back, you can count on that."

As he turned to leave, I kept the gun trained on him until he reached the sidewalk. Then I said, "Oh, and Jethro?"

He said, "Yeah?"

I said, with a smile, "Tell Gibby I hope his kneecap hurts like hell."

#

When I walked through the door to my apartment, Sherry as sitting by the kitchen window, holding the .25 in her tiny hand, and said, "I was watching, in case you needed me."

I said, "Thank you sugar pop."

She said, "He didn't seem like he was just messing around, either."

I said, "No, he wasn't. But I convinced him it was in his best interest to leave."

She smiled and said, "My hero."

I said, "You know it, sugar pop."

She said, "So, what's on the agenda for this evening?"

I said, "Under the present circumstances? I'd say it would be best to lay low, and confine our activities to the apartment."

Sherry looked down at Floof, who was currently rubbing up against her legs and purring up a storm, and said, "What do you think, my Floofy girl?"

The cat purred even louder, and Sherry said, "Floof says she needs more kitty treats."

I said, "That means we will have to *leave* the apartment."

She said, "So? I have my gun, and you have yours. What could go wrong?"

I said, "Plenty."

She said, "Oh, come on, stud puppy. Just down to the corner market and back. It won't take ten minutes."

Against my better judgement, I said, "Well, okay, but let's make it quick."

#

We drove the three blocks to the corner market, and, not seeing any suspicious characters lurking about, we both went inside together to grab the kitty treats.

As we strolled down the aisles, arm in arm, chatting and laughing and sneaking a kiss in the cat food aisle, I felt like a teenager again.

I always felt good when I was with Sherry.

After we hit the checkout lane {the lady at the register flashed me a sour look, like she thought I was a pervert for being with a younger woman} we walked out into the oncoming dusk to see not only a beautiful sunset in the distance, but also saw gap tooth sitting on the hood of my car.

I whispered to Sherry, "Stand *behind* me, and don't make a move unless you have to."

She said, "Okay."

I said to gap tooth, "I thought I had made it clear a how I felt about your company."

Gap tooth grinned and said, "I missed you."

I said, "You won't feel that way much longer, if you don't move your hillbilly ass off my cab."

Gap tooth said, "What if I just take that little pop gun of yours, and shove it down your throat? Then, me and the pretty lady can have some *real* fun."

Sherry said, "I'd rather lick a toilet seat."

Gap tooth said, "Well, that would be a dirty shame, but it can be arranged."

I pulled out the .38, and aimed it waist level at

him, right below his belly button, and said, "Last chance, hillbilly boy."

Then gap tooth slid his big grimy hand into his pocket.

That's when I pulled the trigger on the .38.

Gap tooth went down on his knees, holding his guts and screaming like a banshee. I handed my phone to Sherry and said, "Call Crow. He's on speed dial."

Sherry said, "You're not calling 911?"

I said, "Let Crow do it."

#

As the EMTs loaded gap tooth into an ambulance, Crow walked over to me and said, "Do you know *who* you just sent to the hospital?"

I said, "An asshole?"

Crow said, "Real funny. That was Harley Fox, Gibby's Uncle on his daddy's side."

I said, "Is that supposed to mean something to me?"

Crow said, "It better mean something to you, if you and sweet pants over there want to enjoy your golden years someday."

I said, "I'll be just fine."

Crow said, "Uh huh. Well, I sure wish you could solve your problems in the future without shooting every last member of the Fox family tree."

I said, "They don't have a tree, it's more like a weed, and, he was going for a weapon."

Crow said, "Are you deaf, or just plain stupid?"

I said, "Okay, okay. I'll be a good boy."

Crow said, "I bet you will."

I said, "Do you need me for anything else? My kitty is getting hungry."

Crow said, "Just go home and *stay* there, Milo. Is that clear enough for you?"

I said, "Yes, sir. Right away, sir."

Turning to leave, Crow said, "Smartass."

#

After feeding Miss Floof, Sherry and I sat down at the table and poured us a drink.

As we sat there sipping single malt, Sherry said, "You know, I've been thinking."

I said, "Uh oh. Any time a woman has been *thinking*, there's bound to be trouble."

She said, "Ha ha, Mr smarty pants. Do you want to hear this or not?"

I said, "Sure, go ahead, my dear."

She said, "I think I should just give up my duplex. I'm never going to get caught up on the rent."

I said, "I was already thinking about that, and I have a suggestion."

She said, "Which is?"

I said, "Why don't you move in here – for now, anyway – and save what money you have for later?"

She said, "Why, is my stud puppy suggesting that we become permanent roomies?"

I said, "Yes, I am. But, one big problem remains."

She said, "Which is?"

I said, "You have a whole apartment full of furniture and stuff. What will you do with it?"

Lighting a cigarette, she said, "To be honest, there's not much in there that holds any good memories for me, except my Hello Kitty collection, and an old photo album."

I said, "I got it. We could have a yard sale, and you could make some extra money, and your landlord couldn't keep your deposit that way, either."

She said, "Cool!"

I said, "I have a friednd who has an old pickup truck we could use to haul the furniture over here, I'll give him a call later."

She said, "And in the meantime?"

I grinned and said, "An early dessert?"

She smiled and said, "My thoughts exactly."

So we had dessert.

#

Afterward, as we sat at the table again, sipping cold beer this time, Sherry said, "You know, it's too late to start moving today. Can we do it tomorrow morning?"

I said, "Sure, I haven't called my friend about the truck yet, anyway."

She said, "Milo?"

I said, "Yes, my little sugar pop?"

She said, "Do you *really* want me to move in here? I mean, do you really care for me that much?"

I said, "You wouldn't be here otherwise, my dear."

She said, "I mean, *say* it, Milo. I want to *hear* it."

I cleared my throat and said, "I *want* you to be here."

She said, "And?"

I said, "And, I *love* my sugar pop."

She stood up and sat on my lap, gave me a big kiss, and said, "The feeling is mutual."

I said, "I want to hear it."

She said, "I love my stud puppy."

I said, "You better, because you're stuck with this old fart now."

She said, jokingly, "You're not a fart."

I said, "You're real funny. Better watch out, or I'll give you a good spanking."

Her face lit up and she said, "Oh, I'll be sure to be a bad girl, then."

I said, "Pervert."

She said, "Look who's talking."

#

The next morning I drove to my friend's place to pick up the truck, and left my car there for the time being.

By the time we'd picked up the rest of her stuff and unloaded part of it in the front yard, we were most definitely ready for a cold beer.

As we sat on the front porch steps, sipping cold beer and relaxing, Crow pulled up. Upon seeing his Sedan parking out front, Sherry rolled her eyes and said, "Oh, that's just great."

I said, "Let me handle it."

As Crow approached the front porch, glancing around, he said, "Well, what do we have here?"

I said, "It's called furniture, Crow. People sit on it."

He said, "Real funny. I still think you should be a comedian."

I said, "What you want, Crow? We're busy, and tired."

He said, "Just thought I'd let you know, Harley

Fox came out of surgery just fine. The wound was non lethal."

I said, "He's lucky."

Crow said, "How's it lucky to get a bullet in the gut?"

I said, "I was aiming for his balls."

Crow said, "You're a real class act, you know that, Milo?"

I grinned and said, "I try."

Sherry said, "What *do* you want, Mr Crow?"

Crow said, "Well, ma'am, your..."boyfriend" here, I just wanted to let him know that he won't be going to jail for murder after all."

Sherry said, "Jeez...are you married to someone in the Fox family?"

Crow said, "Great, another comedian."

I said, "What is it with you, Crow? Why are you always dropping by or calling me? Are you related to these inbreds?"

Crow said, "I am just trying my best to make you see how lucky you really are, that I haven't put the cuffs on you yet. But, your luck won't last forever, that's all."

I said, "Duly noted. Is there anything else? We'd like to finish our beer in peace."

Crow said, "I think that'll do for now. Just keep your temper in check, and everything should be fine."

I said, "If you'd keep scumbags like the Fox family off the streets, I wouldn't have to lose my temper."

Turning to leave, Crow said, "Just remember what I said."

Sherry said, "Mr Crow?"

Crow said, "Yes, ma'am?"

Sherry said, "Kiss my ass."

#

The next morning, we were up early, getting ready for the yard sale.

While Sherry sat at the table making price tags for the yard sale items, I began arranging the items outside in the front yard, mostly furniture.

Sherry walked outside as I was taking a break on her old couch, holding the little signs with the prices. She had decorated each one with a cute little drawing of the Hello Kitty cartoon.

She said, "So, what do you think?"

I said, "It should definitely grab their attention."

She said, "You don't think it's too much?"

I said, "I think it's adorable, and I think you are, too."

She blushed and said, "You always know what to say to make me feel good about myself."

I said, "You *should* feel good about yourself. You are special."

With tears of joy in her eyes, she dropped the signs, sat down on my lap, and gave me a big kiss, saying, "The feeling is mutual."

I said, "Well, before we both get too excited to even have a yard sale, we'd better put out the signs, don't you think?"

She said, "Good idea. Go grab us a couple of beers."

I said, "Yes, my Queen. Right away."

#

By around noon, we'd sold just about all of her furniture and other items, except for her old loveseat.

But that was about to change.

Sherry and I had been sitting on the loveseat, sipping beer and sneaking a kiss here and there, when a newer model Mercedes had pulled up out front, one of those cars that practically *screams* rich bitch.

I said to Sherry, "I think we might have just sold the loveseat."

She said, "I hope so. I can use the cash."

I said, "Just leave it to me."

As we stood up, a tall, lean woman with long dark hair climbed out of the Mercedes, glancing around and lighting a thin mint cigar. A lot of wealthy ladies thought the thin mint cigars were a sign of class; to me, they just smelled like a cross between a turd and a Christmas tree.

I'd keep that opinion to myself, of course.

As the woman approached us, we could see she was clad in a very expensive pants-suit, too, the top shining like silk in the sunlight. *Rich.*

As she drew closer, I said, "Good afternoon, ma'am. How can we help you?"

When the woman spoke to us, it was a voice tinged with smoke and liquor, time and rot. Yet, feminine as well. She said, matter-of-factly, "How much for the loveseat?"

Sherry spoke up and said, "Fifty dollars."

The woman cracked a sly grin and said, "Twenty dollars."

I spoke up and said, "Forty dollars." It was always like that, haggling with the wealthy. She most likely did her grocery shopping at the discount food mart.

She said, "Thirty dollars."

Sherry said, "*Fifty* dollars. It's a family heirloom."

Cracking that sly grin again, the woman said, "A family heirloom, huh?"

Sherry said, "Yes, ma'am. My grandmother gave it to my mother, and she gave it to me."

The woman said, "It's not an antique."

I said, "To her, it is. A family heirloom, that is."

The woman said, "Thirty five dollars."

I said, "Forty dollars."

The woman said, "It's not worth that much, and you know it."

I said, "If it isn't worth that much to you, then why are you so intent on buying it?"

The woman said, "That's none of your concern, none of your business."

I said, "It is when some rich bitch is trying to scam me and my girlfriend."

The woman dropped her cigar, stomped it out, and said, "Excuse me?"

I said, "You heard me, Miss fancy pants. You could wipe your ass on money if you chose to, and I bet your brain looks like a cash register."

The woman began to speak, then thought the better of it. She just stood there for a few seconds, eyeballing Sherry and I, like a scientist would look over a lab rat, then she said, ""Forty dollars."

I said, "Deal."

The woman reached into her oversize purse and dug out a wad of cash big enough to choke a bull, and peeled off some bills, handed them to me. She said, "I don't have any way of getting it home. Can you deliver it?"

I said, "All I have is my cab."

She peeled off two more twenties and said, "How about now?"

Taking the money, I said, "What's your address?"

#

After using my buddy's truck again to deliver the loveseat, Sherry and I had retired to my kitchen table to count the cash from the yard sale.

Along with the sale of the loveseat, it added up to almost three hundred dollars. As Sherry sat looking at the money, she said, "Not exactly what I'd expected, but it's better than nothing."

I said, "This is true."

She lit a cigarette and said, "Why do you think she gave in, and paid us what we wanted for the loveseat?"

I said, "She knew that I had her little con game figured out, and knew she couldn't pull a fast one on me, would be my guess."

Sherry said, jokingly, "Damn, and I thought it was my beauty and charm that won her over."

I said, "You can win me over any time, sweet pants."

She said, "Sweet pants? How old are you? Fifteen?"

I said, "Well, you do make me feel young again."

She said, "Fair enough. So, what shall we do with the rest of our day?"

I said, "I think our success with the yard sale calls for a celebration."

She said, "My thoughts exactly! How about a

takeout pizza, some bread sticks, and some red wine?”

I said, “Sounds good to me.”

She said, “*Anything* I suggest seems to sound good to you.”

I said, “It's called being in *love*, babe. Might as well get used to it.”

She said, “Milo, I don't think I can wait for dessert.”

I said, “Me neither.”

#

Later, as we sat on the front porch nibbing on pizza and bread sticks and Floof nibbled on tuna treats, we also watched a beautiful sunset together.

Sunsets in Indiana were something we’d grown to love. The way everything turned to a blinding gold and shined as if it were the only place on the earth. As if the sunset was meant for us alone.

I *wanted* to believe this, so I did.

Sherry did, too.

But, as usual, something would eventually make our bright days dark again, and this time, it was in the form of another visit from Crow.

#

We had been sitting on the porch, sipping red wine and watching Floof chasing squirrels, when a familiar Sedan pulled up out front.

Upon seeing Crow exiting his vehicle, Sherry rolled her eyes and said, “Oh no, not today.”

I said, “Just let me handle him. You stay put and

enjoy your wine."

By the time I reached the sidewalk, Crow was there too, and I said, "So, Mr Crow, to what do we owe another pleasant visit from my favorite cop?"

Crow said, "Go ahead and be sarcastic, but I have good news this time."

I said, "That sounds good. What is it, pray tell?"

Crow said, "Well, it seems like Gibby and Harley Fox have had a change of heart."

I said, "Let me guess; they are both going to give us all a break, and commit suicide?"

Crow said, "I thought you'd be happy to hear that they aren't going to press charges against you."

I said, "What should I do? Open a bottle of champagne, strip down naked, and hop around the front yard like a bunny rabbit?"

Crow said, "There's that sarcasm again."

I said, "And always will be, too. Now, is there anything else you have to tell me before I *try* to enjoy the rest of my evening?"

Crow said, "No, not that I can think of. But if I can come up with anything else, you can count on me to either call or drop by."

I said, "Oh boy, I can't wait."

With that, Crow left, I walked back up to the porch and sat down, and Sherry said, "So? What did Crow have to say this time?"

I said, "He wanted to inform me that neither Gibby or Harley are going to press charges against me."

She said, "Well, that's good thing, right?"

I said, "Not really. I don't see either one of them getting shot, and all of a sudden finding forgiveness for their enemy."

She said, "So, you think it's just a ploy to throw Crow off their trail?"

I said, "I can just about guarantee it."

She sipped her wine and said, "Can we just spend th rest of the evening enjoying ourselves? I've heard enough bad news lately."

Sipping my wine, I said, "Your wish is my command, my Queen."

#

So we did just that.

The next day, we were both up early, taking a drive over to the duplex, to vacuum the rugs, clean the bathroom, etc., so she'd get her damage deposit back.

By around noon, with the place looking pristine, we sat out front and waited for the landlord to drop by.

We didn't have to wait long.

Most landlords make it a point to show up right on time, anxious to find one reason or another to *keep* the deposit, but I was going to make sure that wasn't the case this time.

The landlord, a short, chubby little man with beady eyes and a beer belly, walked through the place, meticulously recording anything in his mind he could deduct from the deposit, and turned to Sherry and said, "That spot there, on the living room carpet? It wasn't there before."

Sherry said, "Yes, it *was*. That's why I had used to have a throw rug laying there, to cover it up."

Beer belly said, "There are still a few nail holes in the living room walls, too. I'll have to pay someone to fill them in."

I said, "No, you won't. I'll take care of that myself."

Beer belly said, "You won't be paid for it."

I said, "I wasn't expecting to be paid."

Beer belly said to Sherry, "The deposit was for three hundred. I'll give you two hundred."

Sherry stood her ground, and said, "No way."

I said, "I can fix those nails holes in ten minutes. It won't cost one hundred dollars, either."

Beer belly said, "And just who are you?"

I said, "Her fiance."

Beer belly said, "No way."

I said, "Yes, *way*. Now, give her the full deposit back, now."

Beer belly said, "I've already made my offer, take it or leave it."

I said to beer belly, "May I speak with you in private for a moment?"

Beer belly shot me a funny look, and said, "I guess so, but make it quick, I'm a busy man."

We walked outside, both of us lighting up a smoke, and he said, "So, what do you want to talk about?"

I said, "I want you to reconsider your offer."

Beer belly said, "Sorry, no can do. I'm a businessman, not a chump. I don't allow a pretty face and a pair of nice legs to sway my business decisions, either."

I said, "Well, it would be in your best interest to do so this time, Mr businessman."

Beer belly said, "And if I choose *not* to do so?"

I stepped closer, almost right in his face, and said, "Then I guess I'll have to *persuade* you to do so."

Beer belly said, "Was that a threat?"

I said, "Are you a cheapskate?"

Beer belly said, "I've made my offer."

I stepped closer again, and grabbed him by the collar of his Polo shirt, pushed him up against the hood of my cab, and said, "And here is my *counter* offer; you give her the *full* deposit back, and you won't be wearing your ass for a hat."

Beer belly said, "You wouldn't dare."

I said, "Try me, asshole. I have kicked ass a lot bigger than yours in the military."

Beer belly took a deep breath, exhaled, and said, "Three hundred it is."

Letting go of his collar, I said, "And she wants it in *cash*."

#

On the way back to my place – well, *our* place – Sherry asked me, "What did you say to him, anyway?"

I said, "I just convinced him it was a good idea to refund your full deposit, that's all."

She said, "I can see that. I meant, *how* did you convince him?

I said, "I just let him know how ridiculous he'd look with his ass on the top of his head."

She giggled and said, "Well, I guess that would do it."

I said, "Now, on with another new day."

She said, "Yes! What shall we do? I'm a rich woman today."

I said, "That's up to you, it's your money, my Queen."

She said, "A shopping trip?"

I said, "Where to, my Queen?"

She said, "Where else? To Walmart and the liquor store!"

#

As we strolled through Walmart hand in hand and sneaking the occasional kiss, I felt better than I had in days.

Young again.

Alive again.

It wasn't just the fact I was arm in arm with a younger woman, either. It was hard to explain, really, but I knew one thing for sure; it didn't matter *how* I'd fallen in love, all that mattered to me was that I *had* fallen in love, and with a young, beautiful, vibrant woman with a heart as big as the moon, who loved me too, and for whatever reason she didn't care either, as long as we were together.

If that makes any sense.

I was hoping it did.

#

When we got back home – *our* home – Floof was waiting anxiously for her tuna treats, happy with her new surroundings as well.

I had always envied, and admired cats and dogs. They loved unconditionally, were loyal and faithful to the end, whereas most humans were not.

Now I had *two* lovely ladies in my life, one human and the other feline, the both of them in love with me unconditionally, and I couldn't ask for more.

I was hoping it would last forever.

Until death do us part.

I hoped.

As we sat down at the table to eat our dinner – cheeseburgers and curly fries and beer – she must have picked up on the fact I had something on my mind.

She said, "Penny for your thoughts, my King?"

I said, "Just thinking about how lucky I am."

She said, "Aw...thank you."

I said, "No, thank *you*."

She said, "Guess what?"

I said, "What, my dear?"

She said, "Next Tuesday is my birthday."

I said, "Is that a hint?"

She said, "Well, A King should buy his Queen a gift for her birthday, don't you think?"

I said, "This is true. What did you have in mind?"

She said, "I don't think you're going to like it very much."

I said, "I won't know until you tell me."

She said, "I was thinking about decorating the bedroom with my Hello Kitty stuff."

I said, "*My* bedroom?"

She said, "Don't you mean *our* bedroom?"

She had me there. "I said, "Okay, *our* bedroom. But, Hello Kitty?" I looked down at Floof when I said it, and she looked up at me like she was thinking, *You might as well give in. The Queen always wins.*

She said, "So? It's no worse than your shower curtain."

My shower curtain had a picture of Norman Bates wearing a dress and holding a bloody knife. I had picked it up at a yard sale because I thought it was funny at the time.

I said, "Okay, but...*Hello Kitty*?"

She said, "It's my *birthday*, Milo."

Floof was right. I may as well give in. I said, "Okay, but, you better do something really *special* for *my* birthday."

Grinning from ear to ear, Sherry said, "Deal."

Thus began my Hello Kitty renovation.

#

We began the renovation before her birthday, so all we'd have to do on that day was celebrate.

Several days later, as I stood back taking it all in at a glance, I had to admit, it was sort of cute, I guess.

But the Helly Kitty pillow shams were a bit much for my tastes.

Did I voice my opinion?

Of course not.

I wanted my special birthday gift, too.

As we stood back admiring our handiwork, she said, "Well, what do you think?"

I said, "Do you *really* want to know?"

She said, "Watch it, Mr smarty pants. I have a gun, you know."

I said, "In that case, I love it."

She said, "I thought so. Now, what shall we do with the rest of our day?"

I said, "Take a nap?"

She said, "No, I mean something that doesn't have to do with the bedroom."

I said, "Take a nap on the couch?"

She said, "No, something that doesn't have to do with sleep."

I said, "Sorry, babe. I'm pooped out."

She said, "Okay, you take a nap and I'll sit on the porch with Floof. It's too pretty outside to sleep the whole day away."

I said, "Deal."

But as it turned out, I wasn't asleep for very long.

#

A short time later, I woke up to the sound of Sherry yelling at someone.

Screaming at them, actually.

I was up from the couch and grabbing my .38 and was already on the porch when I saw Sherry screaming at none other than Gibby Fox, standing there wearing a bloody bandage and a leg brace, and propping himself up with a cane.

She said, "You better get out of here, you piece of shit, or I'll wake up Milo!"

I was standing next to her then, pushing her behind me, as I said to Gibby, "I'm already awake."

Gibby cracked a big goofy grin and said, "Well, if it ain't the big hero, who shoots folks in the kneecap if he can't whup their ass with his fists."

Brandishing the .38 for emphasis, I said, "I don't need a gun, it just heightens my sense of security."

Gibby said, "I was just telling your little sweet tart here, about how much I liked her outfit. You're a lucky man, Milo, but you don't deserve it."

I said, "And I suppose you do?"

Gibby said, "Funny you should say that. Because

I was also telling sweet cheeks here that she needed a *real* man to take care of her, not some low life like you."

I said, "Gibby, you are the lowest form of scum on Earth."

He said, "Oh yeah?"

I said, "Yeah. I've scraped a higher grade of scum off the bottom of my shoes after I walked through a pig pen."

He said, "That hurt my feelings. I think I'm going to cry."

I raised the .38, cocked the hammer back, and said, "You will be crying, if you don't leave the vicinity right now. I'll blow that other kneecap out, and you'll be sitting in a wheelchair on the street corner selling apples."

He said, ""Yeah, and then the rest of my family will take you apart, and feed you to some hogs."

I pointed the .38 right at his head instead, and said, "I'm going to count to *three*."

Sherry said, "Don't bother, just shoot him."

I said, "One..."

Gibby just stood there, leaning on his cane.

I said, "Two..."

He said, "Okay, asshole. I have better things to do, anyways."

I said, "Like what? Kicking puppies?"

He said, "You'll find out soon enough."

Then he turned away, and began hobbling down the sidewalk, mumbling under his breath. Once he was out of sight, I lowered the gun and said to Sherry, "Are you okay?"

She just fell into my arms, as Floof rubbed up against us both, whining loudly. Sherry said, "I'm *scared* this time, Milo. I really am.”

Holding her tight, I said, “I know, babe. I know.”

She said, “So, what now?”

I said, “You just leave that to me.”

Forcing a smile, she said, “I was afraid you were going to say that.”

#

I called Crow, too, just to give him a heads-up.

Needless to say, he was less than thrilled.

When he pulled up out front, Sherry and I were still on the front porch, Sherry just shaking her head in disbelief as I placed my arm around her to console her best I could.

As Crow walked up to the porch steps, I said, “I think the Fox family lied to you.”

Crow said, “No, they didn't, actually. They just said they weren't going to press charges.”

Sherry said, “So, that gives them the right to harrass us at our home?”

Crow said, “No, of course not.”

Sherry said, “And he insinuated that he wanted to sexually assault me, too.”

I said, “And he said he'd be back to pay us a visit, and I doubt it will be a social call, either.”

Crow said, “There's nothing I can do about him *insinuating* something.”

I said, “Just what *can* you do, Crow? Sit on your ass and wait for him to kill one of us?”

Crow said, “I could arrest him for harrassment, or disturbing the peace, but he'd be out of jail in three or four hours.”

I stood up and said, "Crow, I swear, if you don't start doing your job, I'm going to blow his head off."

Crow said, "I *am* going to do something, right now, as a matter of fact."

Sherry said, "It's about time."

Crow said, "Effective immediately, I am placing both of you on house arrest."

I said, "What the hell?!"

Crow said, "That's right. You and your fiance will be restricted to this building, to your apartment, until further notice."

Sherry said, "So, he walks around as free as a bird, while we sit here like prisoners?"

Crow said, "That about sums it up, yes."

I said, "Crow?"

Crow said, "Yeah?"

I said, "Kiss my ass."

Crow said, "No, you will kiss *my* ass. In addition, you will remain under wraps, so to speak, and will not leave this property without my permission, and even then, accompanied by me or another police officer."

I said, "And what is the purpose for this lockdown, if I may ask?"

Crow said, "That way, when one of the Fox family comes on to this property to start any shit, we will have a *legal* reason to arrest him, and he will be held without bail until his court date. *Now* do you understand?"

I said, "I'm beginning to, but I still don't like it."

Sherry said, "Me neither."

Crow said, "It's better than getting injured, or worse, don't you think?"

I had to admit, it was better than seeing my Queen

get hurt – or worse. I said, "Well, alright, but this is still a crock of shit."

Crow said, "I know, Milo, but it's in your best interest for now."

Sherry said, "And what if Gibby comes right into our apartment? In the middle of the night? Then what?"

Crow said, "Then you blow his brains out."

#

Thus began our house arrest.

For the next few weeks, there was no sign of Gibby, or any members of his family, either.

It was as though Gibby and his family could read minds, and knew what Crow had done, and knew not to come on to the property until after the house arrest was lifted – whenever that may have been.

In the meantime, Sherry and I just sat around playing cards or watching TV or taking naps {with one eye open} or, in general, just being bored stiff and pissed off.

It had affected Sherry the most.

She was in a bad mood most days, but tried to hide it from me with a kiss or a smile or a hug, but I knew her heart wasn't in it.

I'd been afraid I was going to lose her altogether.

But we hung in there, and made the best of it, until one day, Crow came by – with some *good* news, this time.

#

We had been sitting at the kitchen table one morning, playing cards and listening to the radio, when Crow knocked on my door.

When I opened the door, Crow was wearing a cocky grin on his face, so I knew it must be good news.

I said, "I haven't seen you smile like that since you lost your virginity."

Crow said, jokingly, "You weren't there when I lost my virginity."

I said, "Just tell me what's so fantastic that it made you actually show some human emotion."

Crow said, "Gibby is in jail being held without bond."

Sherry was there then, and said, "How long will that last?"

Crow said, "Indefinitely for now. He was at the package store around closing time, and the owner wouldn't sell him any liquor. He had a pissy fit and tossed a brick through the front window, almost striking the owner. He's been charged with damage of private property, attempted assault with a deadly weapon, disturbing the peace, and several other charges. He will be getting hard time for this one."

I said, "That's great, but what about Harley? The rest of the Fox clan?"

Crow cracked that cocky grin again and said, "No problem there, either. After I showed the assistant DA all of the paperwork I had on them, she has placed them all on a ten year probation period. If any of them do as much as spit on the sidewalk, it's automatic jail time."

I said, "Well, Crow, I'm actually at a loss for words for a change."

Crow said, "You mean, you ran out of insults to my character for a change."

I said, "Well, that, too."

Sherry's face lit up, and she said, "You mean, no more house arrest?!"

Crow said, "Nope, no more house arrest."

Sherry said, "I would kiss you, but I'm afraid Milo would get jealous."

I said, "Me first."

Crow said, "A simple thank you would be enough for me."

Sherry and I, in unison, said, "Thank you."

Crow said, "You're welcome. Now, I better get back to the office, I have a lot to do."

I said, "Don't be a stranger."

Crow said, "Let's not go too far with your gratitude, Milo."

Then he left.

Sherry looked at me with a big smile, and said, "Shall we celebrate?"

Taking her in my arms, I said, "Dinner or dessert first?"

She said, "You pick."

We had our dessert first.

#

I took her to a *real* restaurant this time.

No burger joints or takeout pizzas. This time, we ate at a restaurant where there was no loud jukebox or rednecks getting in fist fights over a pool game.

Sherry had butterfly shrimp, crab legs, and a salad. I had the same, except with a loaded baked potato on the side.

And, with a bottle of *real* wine, too, not like that cheap stuff at the package store for a dollar ninety nine a bottle.

We had a wonderful time, and I had never seen Sherry so happy.

If my Queen was happy, so was I.

#

On the way home, we felt like we were walking on air, practically floating on it, we were so happy, and when we reached the corner close to our building, we turned that corner to see a small crowd gathered on the front porch, as well as some familiar faces.

Among the crowd was old Miss Edwards, and Willie, among the other faces I was starting to recognize now that I drew closer, the faces of folks that had used my cab company over the last several years.

As Sherry and I walked up to the porch, Willie said, "We all heard the good news, boss. We thought we'd drop by for a visit."

I said, "Good news?"

Willie said, "You know, about the Fox clan being on indefinite hiatus."

I said, "We sure hope so."

Willie said, "We were kinda hoping that now they were out of the picture, you would start driving the cab again."

I said, "I appreciate the sentiment, but I thought everyone was afraid to ride in my cab any more."

Miss Edwards said, "We weren't scared of *you*, Milo. We were scared of *them*."

Sherry stepped forward and said, "I think Milo has decided to retire."

I said, "Yep, I'm seriously considering retiring the taxi service, folks. I'm sorry."

Willie said, "Are you *sure*, Milo? We're really gonna miss you out there."

Looking at all of the sad faces in the crowd, it was hard for me to disappoint them, but I didn't want to disappoint my Queen, either. I finally had a real life to look forward to, and I didn't want to do anything to ruin it, either. Our relationship was my top priority.

I said, "Sorry, folks, but Sherry and I are happy with the way things are now."

Sherry said, "But you folks can come by and visit us any time you want, right Milo?"

I said, "Of course. I wouldn't have it any other way, folks."

That's when everything got real quiet, and the crowd on the front porch slowly began thinning out and walking away, with Willie being the last one to leave.

As he passed by me, he said, "I'm gonna miss you, Milo. Don't be a stranger."

Then he was gone, into the sunset, just a fading shadow among the other shadows of the twilight.

As I stood watching him fade away, I felt as though part of me was fading away with him.

#

Sherry could see it, too.

The sadness in my eyes.

But she didn't say anything – at first.

As the next few weeks turned from Summer to Fall, and the weather kept us inside more often, she had begun to become restless too.

I could see it *her* eyes this time.

But I did say something.

One chilly October night, as we sat at the kitchen table playing cards and sipping single malt, she said, "You really do miss driving the cab, don't you?"

Caught off guard by her remark, I said, "What makes you say that?"

She said, "It's in your eyes, your body language. It's hard not to miss."

I said, "I could say the same about you."

She said, "I'm not sad for me, Milo. I'm sad for you."

I said, "Meaning?"

She said, "Meaning, I know you well enough by now to see that no matter how happy you may be with me, you aren't...complete, I guess. There's something missing, and it's your dream of running the Taxi Land cab company again."

I said, "Is it that obvious?"

She said, "I'm afraid so."

I said, "Please, don't *ever* think it's you. You know I'm happy with you. I've never been this happy before."

She smiled and said, "I know that, silly boy."

I said, "So, if I decided to drive the cab again, only *part time*, mind you, you wouldn't have any problem with it?"

She stood up and sat down on my lap, gave me

one of those sweet little kisses, and said, "If it makes you happy, I'm fine with it."

I said, "Thank you, my Queen."

She said, "Shall we celebrate?"

I said, "Of course."

She said, "Dinner and a movie?"

I said, "How about dinner and then to bed early tonight? I need my sleep if I'm going to drive that cab tomorrow night."

She kissed me again and said, "I think that's a great idea."

#

We didn't wake up the next day until almost noon, when Floof woke us up for some tuna treats.

From there, it was in the shower {both at once, to save time} and on to a late breakfast and a table chat as Floof, now happy as a bug in a rug, lay nearby, snuggling with her new catnip toy.

Taking a bite of eggs, Sherry said, "So, my dear. Tonight is your first night back on the job?"

I said, "Yes, but keep in mind, it's only part time. I have a Queen to take care of."

She smiled and said, "You're so sweet."

I said, "I try."

She said, "You know, I've been thinking about something."

I said, "Which is?"

She said, "Why don't we change the title of your cab service? To something more...colorful? A real attention grabber."

I said, "Go on, I'm listening."

She said, "How about the title, "Sugar Pop" cab company? I think it's quiet catchy."

I said, "I think it's catchy, yes, but doesn't quite scream masculinity."

She said, "Okay, it was just a thought."

I said, "Thank you my love, but I think I best keep it as is."

She said, "So, what nights are you going to work?"

I said, "I was thinking Thursday through Saturday to start. The busiest time of the week for most folks."

Flashing me a sad, puppy dog look, she said, "Couldn't you make it Monday through Wednesday? I'll be awful lonely on the weekends."

Looking into those beautiful green eyes, it was almost impossible to say no. I said, "Okay, it's a deal."

Her face lit up and she hopped on my lap and said, "My hero."

I said, "My Queen."

Then she gave me one of her special kisses, and I don't remember much after that.

#

So, since we now had the weekend to spend together, we'd decided to order a pizza, watch a DVD, and relax.

While we were at the DVD store, looking over our choices {her first choice was a chick flick, and mine was a crime thriller} who else did we run into but Detective Crow, looking over the cop movie selections.

Imagine that?

Upon seeing us walking up the aisle toward him, he smiled and said, "Well, hello, folks. How are we this evening?"

I said, "I don't know about her, but I'm feeling buzzed and ornery." Then I pinched her on the butt.

Her face flushed red as she said, "Milo! Behave yourself!"

Crow just grinned and said, "It's okay, ma'am. I know how he is."

I said, "So, Crow. What brings you out of hiding for one night?"

Crow said, "Worry, mainly, and trying to get my mind off of things."

I said, jokingly, "What would you have to worry about? A famous Detective such as yourself?"

He said, "The wife has cancer. She's only sixty two years old. Breast cancer, in advanced stages."

I felt really bad about giving him a hard time. I said, "I'm so sorry, Crow. Really I am."

Sherry said, "Me too."

Crow said, "Thank you. Well, I best get home and check on the wife. You two have a good night."

Then he turned and walked away without saying another word, not even looking back. I just stood there watching him go, and thought about lucky Sherry and I were to have our health, and each other.

Sherry wrapped her arms around me and said, "Let's go home, Milo. I want to go home."

I said, "Me, too."

#

We spent the rest of the evening just sitting on the couch, watching Floof play with her toys and holding each other tight, and feeling so lucky to be able to do so, and without the dark shroud of death looming over us.

We were still lying there, snuggled up like two cozy kittens, when the sun came up.

#

The next morning, we woke up to the sound of Floof whining and scratching the inside of our front door with her claws.

I climbed off the couch and walked to the door and said, "What's wrong, kitty? What's wrong, Floofy girl?"

She looked up at me, meowed and whined again, and began scratching at the door again. I took a deep breath, exhaled, and opened the door.

There was nobody there.

Just an empty, stuffy hallway, with the first rays of sunlight poking through the building's front windows.

But nothing else to have made a cat throw a pissy fit.

Then I felt it.

A deep, cold chill, down to the bone, making me shiver from head to toe.

Then it was gone.

Floof meowed one more time and took off and hid under the kitchen table.

I closed the door and locked it.

Sherry was awake then, saying, "What's going on, Milo?"

I sat down next to her and said, "Nothing, babe.

Floof was just acting a little weird."

Sherry sat up and said, "How so?"

I said, "She was meowing and scratching at the door, that's all. But there wasn't anybody there."

She said, "Are you sure? Kitty cats are pretty smart, you know."

I said, "Meaning?"

She said, "Meaning, she may have seen – or sensed – something that *you* couldn't see."

I said, "Come again?"

Sherry said, "I'm sure that behind all of that outer beauty, deep down inside, there is much more lurking there other than just color or a soul-less shell beyond that outer beauty."

I said, "You mean, like some type of special power? This is real life, babe, not a scifi movie."

She said, "Well, how else could our beloved pets be so loving and be capable of such amazing things? They know when we are sick and in need of love and affection. They know when we are depressed. Why couldn't they detect when something *weird* is going on?"

I said, "Well, I did feel a cold chill in the hallway, then it was gone."

She said, "See? A cold chill in a *warm* hallway."

I said, "I don't want to talk about this anymore. It's giving me the creeps."

She said, "Okay, babe. I'm sorry."

I said, "Nothing to be sorry about, I'm just not in the mood for anything *sad* or *weird*."

She said, "Fair enough. Now, what shall we do today for entertainment?"

I said, "How about we just play it by ear, and see where the day takes us?"

She said, "A game of cards to begin?"
I said, "Deal."

#

It was around noon when Floof began whining and scratching at the door again.

We'd been playing Uno – and as usual, Sherry was winning every hand – when Floof had suddenly bolted toward the door again, and acting like she had earlier in the day.

I walked over to the door, yanked it open, and once again, there was nobody there.

I closed the door, and before I could reach the kitchen, there was a light rapping on the door, and I walked back and yanked it open to see Willie standing there, his face solemn and his eyes wet and bleary.

I said, "Damn, Willie, you don't look so good."

He said, sadly, "There's something I think you should know, Milo."

Almost dreading to hear what he had to say, I said, "I'm listening."

He said, "Crow is dead."

Totally taken back by his remark, I said, "Come again?"

He said, "Late last night, I guess. He gave his wife a fatal injection of Phenol, and then he shot himself. One of his neighbors heard the gunshot and called the police."

Sherry was there then, her eyes wet with tears as well. She said, "Oh my God. We just saw him at the video shop last night."

Willie said, "I'm sorry, folks, really I am. I just

thought you'd want to know."

I said, "Well, I appreciate it, Willie. Is there anything else?"

Willie said, "Not right now, no. Well, I better get going. I have the strongest feeling I'm going to end up drunk today."

I said, glumly, "You and me both."

#

A short time later, as we sat at the table playing Uno again, Sherry couldn't concentrate on the game any more than I could.

After a few minutes of a sad silence, I said, "It's going to be okay, babe. We can get through this."

She said, "I know. It's *so sad*."

I said, "Yes, it is, but, we have to move forward, babe. Crow wouldn't want us to sit around and feel sorry for him. He made his choice."

She said, "I know that, but it's still so sad and negative."

I said, "To Crow, it was an act of *mercy* for his wife."

She said, "But why shoot himself?"

I said, "He probably couldn't handle the fact that he was the one who took her life. Maybe it was a feeling of guilt."

She said, "Either way, it's just so damn *depressing*."

I said, "Let's not think about this all day. How about a drink?"

She said, "I could use *a lot* of drinks."

I said, "Me, too. How about some single malt?"

She said, "*Yes*, please."

#

We ended up so blasted, I woke up on the kitchen floor, and Sherry woke up on the bathroom floor – after she had voided her stomach, of course.

We had spent the rest of that day trying our best to recuperate, although it was a rough road back to sobriety.

I had forgotten how much damage a large bottle of scotch could do to someone, let alone two someones.

After we'd spent some time guzzling black coffee and popping pain relievers, we'd ended up in bed for the rest of the day, snuggled up like cozy kittens, with Floof lying between us, purring up a storm.

It was that day I realized just how much smarter cats were than people gave them credit for, too.

#

We both woke up around midnight, and, not being able to go back to sleep, we'd decided to stay up and take a long hot shower to sober up some more.

We both felt a bit better after the shower, although still a bit weak. We had decided to snuggle up on the couch, and watch the movie we'd rented the other night, although we couldn't really concentrate on it.

We woke up early in the morning, with the DVD player still on, making a funny humming noise, but both of us feeling better this time.

But although our bodies felt better, our minds were still racing with ghastly visions of Crow injecting his wife with a lethal dose of Phenol, and then, blowing his own brains out.

We were drinking single malt again by noon.

#

It was Monday.

In my alcohol induced haze, I had forgotten I was supposed to drive the cab that night.

As Sherry sat at the kitchen table swilling black coffee, I hopped in the shower real quick, doing my best to sober up before my shift. Floof just laid close by, playing with a catnip toy, oblivious to any human problems.

I'd always envied cats, living a life of luxury, just laying around looking cute and getting waited on hand and foot by the humans. That Monday morning, I wished I was a kitty, and I could stay home and curl up on Sherry's lap and be loved on all day.

That is, if Sherry could sober up long enough.

As I sat down at the table to slip my shoes on, I said, "You don't look so good."

She said, "Wow, thanks a lot, Mr romance."

I said, "I didn't mean to offend you, my love. I'm sorry."

She said, "It's okay, I know that. So, I gather you're going to drive the cab tonight?"

I said, "I'm going to try to, anyway. I'm not sure how long I'll last."

She said, "Will you be terribly upset if I stay home? I'm just not up to it."

I said, "I wasn't going to invite you along,

anyway. I figured you could use the rest."

She said, "Thank you. Would you do me a favor, though?"

"Sure," I said, lighting a cigarette. "Name it."

She said, "Come by now and then and check on me? It would make me feel better."

I said, "You got it. Anything else?"

With teary eyes, she said, "I could use a hug right now."

I said, "Me too." I hugged her, more tightly than ever before, and she sobbed a little, her face buried in my chest, as she let it all out.

She said, "I'm sorry. I'm a big baby, I know."

I said, "It's okay, I shed a few tears myself lately."

She said, "Does it ever stop?"

I said, "What's that?"

She said, "The hurt. The *pain* of it all."

I said, "No, it doesn't. As long as you have a good, pure heart, caring about other's misfortune and misery comes with the territory."

She said, "Yeah, I guess so."

I said, "Well, I better go gas up the cab and grab some smokes for the road. "Need anything?"

She said, jokingly, "A new liver?"

I said, "I'll see what I can do."

#

As I stood at the gas pumps, filling up the tank, my train of thought was suddenly broken by the sound of Willie's voice coming up behind me.

I turned to see Willie weaing that *look* he gets, the one he gets when he has something *bad* to tell me.

He said, "Just wanted to let you in on a vicious rumor I heard last night."

I said, "Well, spill the beans. I feel like shit already, so I guess it doesn't really matter."

He leaned in and said, "I was at the Third Base tavern last night, using the bathroom facilities, when I overheard a conversation between Harley Fox and his half brother, Billy Charly."

I said, "And?"

Willie said, "Harley was offering Billy money to put the hurts on you. I guess the whole family took up donations to see you get your ass kicked."

I said, "It figures, with Crow out of the way, and hiring Billy Charly, too. He most likely isn't listed on the probation order."

Willie said, "Pretty smart of them, for a bunch of inbred hillbillies."

I said, "Yeah, well, I'm pretty smart, too."

Willie said, "This is true. But, I'd still be watching my back, if I were you."

I said, "Thanks for the heads up, Will."

He said, "Any time."

#

I drove to the quick mart next, to pick up some cigarettes for Sherry and I.

As I walked outside, I saw an older woman, about sixty-ish, sitting on the hood of an older model Buick, puffing away on a dog turd cigar. She looked right at me, well, *glared* right at me, like her beady little eyes were burning a hole right through my soul.

She said, "I thought that was you."

I said, "Excuse me?"

She said, "I said, you're the one who shot my grandson. I recognized you, alright."

I said, "Which one? I shot two of them."

She said, "Smartass little prick, ain't you?"

I said, "I do my best."

She said, "You look...*different*, now. Don't look so good. I always heard a guilty conscience will do that to a man."

I said, "I sleep just fine."

She said, "Yeah, most chickenshit assholes do sleep like a baby. They don't know any better, believe they've done carried out a righteous act of violence."

I said, "It *was* righteous. It wasn't my fault they were dumb enough to bring a knife to a gunfight."

She said, "They didn't. I heard you set them up."

I said, "It was justified."

She said, "That what they call it now? Justified? He had a knife, you had a gun. Wasn't no contest there. Besides, I know my grandson. He was just blowing smoke up your ass, acting all tough. He wouldn't have *really* hurt your girlfriend. He just wanted you to *think* he would have."

I said, "He should have thought about that before he decided to act like an asshole. Is there anything else you have to say? I'm busy."

She said, "Yeah, I'd be watching my back, if I was you."

Climbing into the cab, I said, "Will do. Oh, and tell Billy Charly I got a bullet with his name on it."

#

I drove way past the speed limit back to my apartment.

When I burst through the door, Sherry was sitting on the couch watching the Weather Channel, and she sat bolt upright, startled by my loud entrance.

She said, "What's wrong, Milo?!"

I said, "I just wanted to make sure you were okay, that's all."

She said, "Don't bullshit me, Milo. What's going on?"

I sat down next to her and said, "I ran into Willie at th gas station. He told me that some guy named Billy Charly is out for me."

She said, "Oh no, not again."

I said, "It's nothing to worry your pretty little head about. I've got it under control. But, I do want you to do me a favor."

She said, "Let me guess. Keep that gun by my side at all times."

I said, "Good girl."

I handed her a pack of smokes and said, "Better get going, if I'm going to make any money."

She said, "You mean, if you're going to find this Billy guy and shoot him, right?"

I said, "Not unless he makes me shoot him."

She said, jokingly, "Then he's most likely a dead man already."

#

I ended up cruising the North end for a while, searching every last alley way, under every rock, nook, and cranny a low life like Billy Charly could be hiding from plain sight.

Then again, I didn't even know what he looked like, either.

So, I drove to the Union bar and grill, a local hangout for local dirtbags, to see if anyone knew of his whereabouts.

When I walked into the bar, almost every last bar patron stopped what they were doing, stared at me like I was an alien from another galaxy, then went back to what they were doing; drinking, smoking, puking, or just being a low life in general.

I walked up to the bar to see the so called bartender, a tall, lanky fella with a scar over his right eye wiping the bar down with a dirty rag. I lit a smoke and placed my lighter on the bar.

I leaned in and said, "You the bartender?"

He said, "Sort of."

I said, "Good enough. Do you know a fella by the name of Billy Charly?"

He said, "Yeah. What about him?"

I said, "I heard he is looking for me."

He said, "Oh yeah? Well, I wouldn't worry too much about it."

I said, "Why is that?"

He said, "Because he's a punk, that's why. Unless he has a knife or a gun, he's harmless."

I said, "And if he *does* have a weapon?"

He said, "Then, you better hope *you* have a weapon. He's one crazy son of a bitch, when he drinks, too. If he's drunk and packing a weapon, you'd best hope you have the chance to sneak up behind him."

I said, "Oh yeah?"

He said, "*Yeah*. He's one sly, sneaky little bastard, too."

I said, "Yeah, well, so am I."

He said, "Well, this should be a very interesting situation, then, huh?"

I said, "I'm sure it will be. You happen to know where I might find him?"

He said, "Just look in every shithole you can find, and he most likely won't be too far away."

I said, "Imagine that."

I began to walk away when the bartender said, "If I should see him, want me to relay a message for you?"

I said, "Yeah. Just tell him that Milo Burress has a bullet waiting for him, with his name on it."

The bartender said, "Will do."

#

After leaving the bar, I drove by my place again, to check on Sherry – and Floof the cat, of course.

They were curled up on the couch together, watching the Animal Planet channel, some show about cutest kittens. Floof was staring at the TV screen and purring up a storm, as if she knew what was going on. Sherry was right; cats are smarter than folks give them credit for.

When I walked in, she said, "So, did you have any luck finding your most recent nemesis?"

I said, "Nemesis might be pushing it, but no, not yet. How are you and Floof doing?"

She reached down beside her, and pulled out the small .25 auto, and said, "Just fine."

I said, "Good girl."

She smiled and said, "Always."

I said, "Mind if I hang out with you ladies for a little while? I'm getting bored just driving around."

Sherry said, "Sure! I was missing you anyway. I need a big bear hug from my King."

I sat down next to her, and said, "And I need a big kiss from my Queen."

So, we shared a big hug and smooch, Floof purred her approval, and we sat watching the Animal Planet.

#

About two hours later, we were still watching TV.

I had suddenly lost all interest in finding Billy Charly, and just wanted to be close to my two most important ladies, where I felt safe and happy again.

But as usual, my happiness was short lived at best.

#

I had forgotten my Zippo cigarette lighter at the Union bar.

It was only a lighter, but I'd had it since my military days, so it most definitely had sentimental value.

After making sure that Sherry and Floof were tucked in as snug as a bug in a rug, I'd driven back to the Union bar. Upon walking in, I noticed that the guy who'd been the bartender earlier in the evening wasn't there, and had been replaced with a short, stocky fella whose general appearance just screamed *bar owner.*

I walked up to the bar and said to him, "Excuse me, but where is the guy that was here earlier?"

The guy said, "Oh, he's already gone home. He just fills in sometimes when I make a bank run."

I said, "Do you happen to know if he found a Zippo lighter on his shift?"

The guy said, "It would be easy enough to find out." He walked over to the cash register area, picked up an old cigar box, and peeked inside. Then he pulled out my Zippo and said, "Is this it?"

I said, "Oh yeah. Thank you so much for holding it for me."

He came back and placed the lighter on the bar and said, "Thank Billy. He's the one who found it."

I said, "Last name? I'd like to thank him in person sometime."

The guy said, "Charly. His name is Billy Charly."

My blood ran cold as I ran back to my cab, hopped in, and drove as fast as I could back to my place.

Our place.

#

I pulled up out back, in the dark, so I couldn't be seen snooping around the windows.

I crept up to the back door, my .38 in hand, and took a quick peek inside. My heart almost burst through my chest at the sight of Sherry sitting at the kitchen table, holding Floof close to her chest, and Billy Charly sitting across from her, holding a beer in one hand and a huge knife in the other.

I took a deep breath, exhaled, and slowly, gently, began pushing the back door open.

Billy sat there hurling threats and insults at Sherry, but I heard none of that. My mind was concentrated soley on blowing his brains out.

As the inside door creaked open, Sherry saw me then, but showed no reaction, knowing what I intended to do.

Within seconds, I was standing right behind Charly, and was aiming the gun right at his head.

That's when I winked at Sherry, giving her the signal to stand up. Upon seeing her stand up, Charly said, "Hey, bitch. Where do you think you're going?"

Sherry said, "I'm going to the bathroom, you asshole, but you're going to the morgue." Then she ran down the hallway to the bathroom, and locked herself inside.

That's when I pressed the end of the gun barrel against the back of his head, and cocked the hammer back.

He instantly froze as stiff as a statue, his whole body locked up so tight, he wouldn't even be able to fart.

He cleared his throat and said, "Now, just take it easy there, buddy. Don't do something you're gonna regret."

I said, "The only thing I regret right now is the fact I didn't blow your half brother's brains out while I had the chance. But I might just rectify that tonight."

Charly said, "You shoot me, my whole family will be coming for you."

I said, "Good, I can shoot them all at at one time, save some gas money."

Charly must have realized I wasn't just messing

around, because he said, "Listen, hoss. We can work something out."

I said, "Too late for that. You mess with my lady, you have already crossed over that barrier between just being an asshole, and being a *dead* asshole."

Charly said, "Please, man, just give a me break. You won't ever see me again, I promise."

I said, "You got that right. You'll be in the ground soon enough, taking the long dirt nap."

That's when Charly, in one last pitch effort to save his own rotten ass, began to swing the knife around at me, at waist level.

That's when I pulled the trigger.

As what little brains he had splattered my kitchen walls, I said, "And that's what happens when you bring a knife to a gunfight, dumbass."

#

A little while later, as the EMTs and the coroner took care of Charly's remains, one of the police officers, a Deputy Kent Jacobs, walked up to me and said, "Well, it's a clear case of self defense, that's for sure. How is the lady doing? Sherry, is it?"

I said, "Yes, Sherry. She's okay, just shaken up a bit. She is lying down right now."

Jacobs said, "I imagine she needs the rest. Do me a favor, and let me know when she'd be available to answer a few questions, okay? It's just normal procedure."

I said, "Will do. Anything else you need? I have brains to clean up."

Jacobs looked kinda sick and said, "No, I think

that's all for now."

I said, "Good. I've already had enough bullshit for one day."

#

After everyone was gone, and my neighbors had finally stopped snooping around with their cell phone cameras, I went back inside to clean up the mess in my kitchen, to find Sherry on her knees, wiping up brains off the linoleum floor.

I said, "Babe, please, let me take care of that. I think you've been through enough for one night."

Wiping sweat from her face, she said, "It's fine, Milo. I'm almost done, anyway."

I said, "You shouldn't have to do that."

She said, jokingly, "Then you should watch your temper."

I said, "Fair enough."

She stood up, wrung the bloody washrag out in a plastic bucket, and said, "So, what shall we do for the rest of the night? Go find another member of the Fox family and have some target practice?"

I said, "Don't tempt me. But I do need to make one short trip, if you don't mind."

She said, "Oh no, now who are you going to shoot?"

I said, "Nobody. I just want to have an important chat with someone."

She said, "I don't really feel like being alone right now, Milo."

I said, "I already thought of that. I'll ask Miss Vivian upstairs if you can sit with her while I'm gone.

She is very sweet, and she loves kitty cats."

Reluctantly, Sherry said, "Well..okay, but please don't be gone too long."

I said, "Deal."

#

After I was sure Sherry and Floof were tucked away safely at Miss Vivian's place, I drove to the Union bar.

I didn't bother trying to be sneaky about it, either. I parked right out front – on the sidewalk – and when I burst through the front doors like John Wayne, with my trusty .38 visible in the front of my waistband, you could have heard a pin drop.

All of the bar patrons, men and women alike, just sat staring at me, like I was a ghost, and to them, I most likely seemed like a ghost, because I was supposed to be dead.

I walked up to the bar to see the same guy who'd been there earlier staring at me like he was about to shit himself. I said, "Just thought I'd let you know, your part time bartender won't be coming back. He had a thirty eight caliber lobotomy several hours ago."

The guy said, nervously, "Well, thanks for letting me know."

I said, "Now, get out from behind the bar, and stand out here where I can see watch you."

He said, "Come again?"

I pulled out the .38, cocked the hammer back, and said, "Now, dipshit. Don't make me repeat myself."

The guy walked out from behind the bar, and stood close to the jukebox. Then I turned to face the crowd and said, "Well, is there *anybody* here that isn't a member of the Fox family tree?"

Nobody said a word. Imagine that.

I said, "If there is anybody here that wants a piece of me, actually has the guts to speak up, do it now. Let's get this over with."

Again, no word or reaction from anyone, just a room full of blank stares and whispered secrets.

I stepped forward and said, "The next time some asshole comes after my lady – or me – I'm going to *blow their damn brains out*, whether they are related to the Fox family or not. Is that clear?"

No reaction again from the crowd, which was a good thing, really; I didn't have to turn the bar room into a blood bath.

I said, "Yeah, that's what I thought, a room full of cowards, a bunch of inbred retards. You can *all* go to hell."

Then I turned around and left, before I did something I might actually be sorry for – but that was doubtful.

#

When I got back to my place, Sherry was already back home, sitting on the couch with Floof, watching the local news.

I said, "I thought I told you I wanted you to stay up at Miss Vivian's place until I came home."

She turned to me and said, "I was bored, so I came back here. A girl can only take so much of hearing about someone's thimble collection."

I said, "Fair enough. Did you have your gun with you?"

She reached down and produced the .25, smiled, and said, "Yes, my King."

I said, "Good girl."

She said, "So, did you have your little chat?"

I sat down next to her, and said, "For what little good it may have done, yes."

She said, "That doesn't sound good."

I said, "It is what it is."

She said, "By the way, you're famous now."

I said, "How so?"

She said, "It was on the local news already, about you shooting Billy Charly."

I said, "And just how does that make me famous?"

She said, "Well, the news lady on TV, she said you would be a hero now, taking down some of the biggest criminal family in the city."

I said, "Oh, that's just great. Now I *will* be a target for sure."

She said, "I doubt it. I think you finally got your point across."

I said, "I hope so, because I want to live my life, with you, and not have to be looking over my shoulder."

She said, jokingly, "I think you would look cute with eyes in the back of your head."

I said, "And I think you would look cute in your birthday suit, too."

She said, "Is that a hint?"

I said, "Am I the local hero?"

She hugged me and said, "You are *my* hero, Mr Milo Burress, and that's good enough for me."

I said, "Then let's see that birthday suit."

#

Over the next few weeks, I had begun to feel like a local hero, despite of my protest.

I had only done what I had wanted to believe anyone in my situation would do; stand up to those who would rob or hurt or even kill innocent people.

Yet, I had news crews at my door, wanting to interview me, and was followed around the grocery store like a celebrity, and a couple of people had even asked me for my autograph.

I enjoyed the attention, I guess. But all I wanted mostly was to live my life in peace – with my lady.

My Queen.

And Floof, of course.

#

One day, as I sat on the front porch with Sherry, on an unseasonably warm November evening, watching the sun go down, an unfamiliar car pulled up out front, and out climbed Kent Jacobs, the cop that had responded to Billy Charly's long dirt nap.

As he exited the small Sedan and walked up to the porch, I said, jokingly, "Do all cops drive Sedans off the clock?"

He smiled and said, "It's a company car, and it saves me gas money."

I said, "Fair enough. So, what brings you out tonight?"

He said, "I may have an offer you can't refuse."

I glanced at Sherry, she shrugged her shoulders, and I said, "Is that good or bad?"

He said, "That may depend on how you look at it."

I glanced at Sherry again, and we both shrugged our shoulders, and I said, "Well? We're waiting."

He said, "I am here to offer you a position."

I said, "As what? A target practice dummy?"

He laughed and said, "No, as an interim Sheriff for the county."

Sherry said, "Wouldn't that be sort of a dangerous position, under the circumstances?"

He said, "Not really. Your fiance has already seen to that."

I said, "How so? Did the Fox family tree suddenly burn down?"

Jacobs cracked a grin and said, "It might as well have. Their granny, the one you apparently had a conversation with? She dropped dead from heart failure upon hearing about Billy Charly's demise. Gibby will most likely die in prison. Harley just found out he has cancer of the testicles."

Sherry grinned and said, "Karma can be a real fickled bitch."

I said, "That sort of taints the family blood line, doesn't it?"

Jacobs said, "Yes, thank God."

I said, "So, why me for interim Sheriff?"

He said, "A lot of the folks around here sent a petition to city hall, requesting your services. They couldn't think of anyone better qualified to take the position."

I said, "I'm flattered, but I'm no cop."

Jacobs said, "You are former military, decorated. You know your way around guns, and most of all, you don't take any unnecessary shit."

I said, "Well, that's true." I glanced over at Sherry again, and she just shrugged her shoulders indifferently. I said to Jacobs, "Can I get back to you on this?"

He said, "Sure, take your time, and just let me know."

As he turned to walk away, I said to Sherry, "So, my love. What do you think?"

She said, "I think this is just another way for you to get killed by some homicidal maniac."

I said, "Wow, I'm glad you have so much faith in me."

She said, "I didn't mean it *that* way, Milo. But you'll have to admit, we've had enough excitement around here for now, don't you think?"

I said, "I can't argue with that."

Sherry said, "But, I also want you to be happy, too, so I feel like I'm stuck between a rock and a hard place."

I said, "Why don't we just forget about this for now, and spend the rest of the night relaxing and enjoying ourselves? We can talk about this some other time."

She smiled and said, "Thank you, dear. I feel better already."

I said, "So, what shall we do? It's getting a little chilly out here now."

She said, "How about some fortified coffee and a game of Uno?"

I said, "How about single malt scotch and no coffee? And you always beat me at Uno."

She grinned and said, "That's because you always have something naughty on your mind when we play cards."

I said, "Guilty as charged."

#

After I lost at Uno again, we had decided to hit the sack early, get a good night's sleep. We had planned a shopping trip for the next day, and I wanted to be as fresh as a daisy the next morning – or that is, what might pass for daisy fresh, anyway.

The next morning, after a long hot shower and some strong coffee, we'd headed out to the nearby shopping mall, to look at some new Hello Kitty items for Sherry, and some single malt and various food items for the both of us.

As we strolled through the liquor aisle, a lady who'd been looking over the bourbon selection suddenly glanced over at us and said, "You're him, aren't you?"

I said, "Excuse me?"

She said, "I'm sorry, but aren't you Milo Burress, the guy who shot Billy Charly?"

I said, glumly, "Yes, that was me."

Sherry broke in and said, "And you are?"

The lady said, "My name is Audrey Meadows. My son, William, was stabbed by Billy Charly years ago, and he died. He was only eighteen years old. I couldn't wait for the day that Charly got what was coming to him."

I said, "I'm so sorry, ma'am."

She said, "But thanks to you, he's in a grave, where he belongs, and his family has been taken apart."

I said, awkwardly, "Well, I'm glad I could make things better for you."

She said to Sherry, "You have a brave man there, my dear. You should be proud."

Sherry wrapped her arms around me and said, "Oh, believe me, I am."

The lady said, "Well, I better get going, but you two have a wonderful day."

After the lady had walked away, Sherry said, "So that's what it's like to be a real hero."

I said, "I'm no hero."

Sherry said, "You're *my* hero."

I said, "Well, there's that."

She kissed me on the cheek and said, "Let's go home, my hero. We have things to talk about."

#

As we stored our purchases away – all except for the single malt, that is – Sherry said, "So, my hero, I guess you really are famous now."

Pouring two glasses of scotch, I said, "Yeah, and that particular position also comes with a lot of responsibility to maintain it."

She said, "So, you have decided not to accept Jacob's offer?"

I said, "I had the impression that you weren't too crazy about the idea."

She sat down at the table and said, "That's because I wasn't seeing the full picture yet."

I said, "Which is?"

She said, "Well, you have to admit, you get really bored at times. I don't mean with me, I mean with not driving the cab any more. And you'll have to admit, being able to get out and drive around, and serve the town at the same time, does sound appealing to you, right?"

I said, "Well, it does sound fun."

She sipped her drink and said, "I just have to get used to sharing my hero with the community part of the time, that's all."

I said, "Are you serious?"

She said, "As a heart attack."

I said, "Did I ever tell you that I love you?"

She said, "Not very often, but I know you do, Mr tough guy."

I said, "I love you, my Queen."

She said, "I love you too, my King."

At that very moment, when we stood and embraced, sharing a passionate kiss, I *knew* we were going to be together forever.

#

The next day, around noon, Jacobs swore me in as the new interim Sheriff.

As we stood on the front porch, with some of my neighbors and old friends in attendance, and Sherry by my side, my Queen, I was sworn in.

Afterward, we all had a short but sweet celebration, and then Sherry and I retired to the bedroom, where we had our own *private* celebration.

It was the best day of my entire life.

That is, until the day Sherry and I were married.

#

It was the following Spring, on a bright, warm, sunny day in April, when Sherry and I tied the knot.

It was just a small, semi-private ceremony, with mainly just old friends in attendance; Willie, Miss Edwards, and the honorable Pastor Ron Kerr.

We spent our honeymoon at home, and it was just fine with us, and Floof of course, who insisted on sleeping with us that night, to get her share of love and affection, too.

Unconditional love.

What more could I ask for?

#

One beautiful warm day in May of that year, as Sherry and I sat on the front porch watching Floof playing with her new catnip mouse, Sherry had asked me a question that threw me off at first, but after I'd mulled it over, didn't seem all that odd after all.

Sipping her wine and gazing at the oncoming sunset, she said, "You know, I never had stopped to think about it until now, that the lights up in the sky, have to be billions of years old by the time we see it, from the beginning of time right past us, into the future."

I said, "Maybe they're souls, traveling through starlight, searching for homes."

She said, "Do you really believe that?"

I said, "How can I not believe in it? You and me found each other, didn't we?"

She said, "You're right, I'm sorry. Sometimes I just get paranoid, I guess."

I said, "No reason to be paranoid. Look back at the last few months. The most danger I've been in has been breaking up a fight at the local bar, or writing parking tickets."

She said, "I know."

I said, "Then let's not spend our evening like this. How about we go out for dinner?"

She seemed to perk up then and said, "Do I get to pick the place?"

I said, "Sure."

She said, "How about Mexican food? I love Mexican food."

I said, "You never told me you love Mexican food before. How come?"

She said, "Because I know Mexican food gives you indigestion and gas."

I said, "You're silly."

She said, "But you love me, though."

She was right about that. I said, "Come here, my little love bug, and give me some of those good hugs and kisses."

Sitting on my lap and smothering me with kisses, she said, "There. Think that will satisfy your cravings for now?"

I smiled and said, "Until it's time for dessert."

She said, "You're silly."

I said, "But you love me though, don't you?"

She said, "Yes, my King, always."

I smiled and kissed her cheek, stroking her hair as she curled into me. She fell asleep in my arms, and I knew she'd dream of our love.

We never made it to the Mexican restaurant.

David Boyer is a Christian, a multi-genre writer, a true crime buff, and the author of several coming of age novellas, numerous horror and scifi stories, as well as the author of numerous essays including the subjects of government corruption, Christianity, bullying, and cyber-stalking.

He lives in Vincennes, Indiana, with his cat, Holly Jean, who now serves as his copy editor by jumping on the computer keyboard when he's not looking.

Books: {Non-fiction}
True crime:
Small Town Murder: True Crime Stories From Knox County, Indiana
Murder In the Hoosier Heartland: Infamous Indiana Murderers & Fledgling Serial Killers
Murder & Mayhem In the Hoosier Heartland: Mysterious Disappearances & Bizarre Murders In Indiana
The Blitz: A Rape Victim's Story
Vanished In Vincennes: the Mysterious Disappearance and Death Of Dolores Oliver
47 Years of Hell: The Dolores Oliver Murder: Still Unsolved
Small Town Murder In Knox County, Indiana: Hate Crimes, Witch Hunts, and A Definitive List of Indiana Serial Killers
The Guy In The Blue Shirt

Non-fiction: {paranormal, bio & memoir}
Haunted Heartland: Haunted Hoosiers Tell Their Ghost Stories
Strange Happenings In the Hoosier Heartland
I Remember When, In Vincennes...Volume 1
Growing Up In Vincennes – Volumes 2 – 5
The Time of Our Lives: Growing Up Cool In Vincennes, Indiana

Essays:
Bullying: the Road to Recovery and Forgiveness
Privacy In the Age of the Internet: How Sexting and Sharing Private Photos Can lead To Cyber-Stalking

Once An Alcoholic, Always An Alcoholic? The Cold Hard Truth About Our Addictions
Travesties of Jutice: Flaws In Our Legal System That Imprison the Innocent
Will the REAL Christian Please Stand Up?
Racism in the 21st Century: ALL Lives Matter
Conflicted Souls: How the Man In Black Saved My Life
Crossing the Rainbow Bridge: Saying Goodbye To Our Beloved Pets

Books: {Fiction}
Mystery, Indiana
Human Sawdust

Stories: {Long fiction, novellas}
Mystery, Indiana
The Mind of Luther Biggs
LUTHER
Jenny
Lester Talbot and His Magic Eye
Beautiful Ghosts
Pretty Flamingo
Jack and Norma Jean
The Things We Leave Behind – Volumes 1 – 3
Ghosts of Summer
Gardens
Claustrophobia
The Cemetery Artist
Brain Pie
Beast
The Jailhouse Movie Star
Easy Pickings
The Dominant Thumb
Joyride
The Maverick
Freak
Grandma's Gooseberry Pie
Dancing With the King

Always In My Heart
Hillbilly Moonshine Zombies
Home
Sheva
A Debt Repaid In Full
The Enlightening Darkness
The Good Neighbor
Wander
The Hungry Ones
A Gunfighter's Legacy
Dead Man's Hand
Inhuman Experiments – Part 1, 2, and 3
Jennifer
Spider Bait
Goodnight, My Love
Poor Larry
Creepy Crawl
The Ballad Of Georgie

Other recent book releases by David Boyer
{Now available on Lulu.com}

Dolores Oliver, fondly nick-named 'Lert' by her friends as a term of endearment, was out an out-going and friendly woman who was well liked by all who knew her.

Yet, on September 7, 1974, while on a visit to a local bar to chat with friends, she simply vanished without a trace. Foul play was immediately suspected by her family, who knew in their hearts that they could think of absolutely no one who would want to do her any harm.

Yet her lifeless body was found at the end of October in a bean field by a farmer in Illinois. Lawrence County coroner Dale Nichols was able to make a positive ID through dental records and a ring Mrs Oliver was wearing.

Who would have done such a thing, and why? Hopefully, VANISHED IN VINCENNES will help to finally solve one of the oldest cold cases in Indiana, and bring her family some closure they have sought for so long.

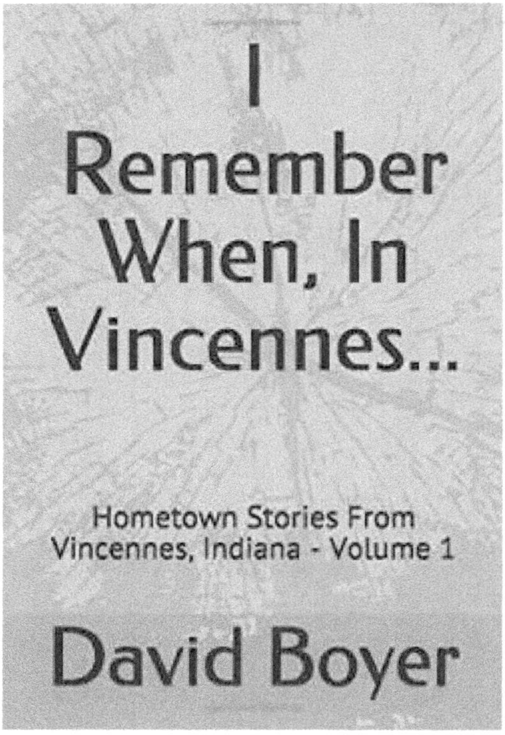

Unfortunately, even small towns – Vincennes included – eventually change, sometimes for the better, and other times, not so much. It's the natural order of things.

Trees grow old and fall. Sidewalks split and crack and are replaced for public safety's sake. Old houses – and all the memories associated with them – are demolished and replaced with parking lots or duplexes. Even historical landmarks, Mother Nature and Father Time having taken their toll, sadly, vanish – except for our own pictures and memories of them.

Luckily for Vincennes residents, local historian Norbert Brown has created a Facebook group page entitled, *Vincennes Remember When*, to help all of us keep our fond memories intact, and to reminisce and enjoy them 24-7.

It was his infinite wisdom of our local history and group page that was the inspiration for this book – and the stories within. Some of these stories may elicit a tear, some laughter.

Some may remind you of an old friend you haven't seen since high school – or, sadly, one that has passed in recent years. Some may remind you of your childhood, your teenage years – or having to bid them farewell, in order to move on to bigger and better things; marriage, children, grandchildren, and a lifetime of wonderful memories that only a tight-knit, loving family can provide.

It is my sincere belief that there will be a story for *everybody* within these pages, regardless of whether you may be a Vincennes history buff or not.

As of 2015, it is believed that there are at least 200 serial killers active in the United States at any given time.

33 of them were from Indiana.

Nobody in their own home town would have wanted to imagine a fledgling {or full fledged} serial killer lurking about, searching for his next victim. Or imagine one being their next door neighbor or the relative of a friend or even attending the local college.

Yet, since the early 1970s, Vincennes, Indiana, Knox County, and Indiana in general has had it's share of cold blooded murder.

It's really sad – as well as terrifying – to even imagine all these brutal, cold blooded murders have taken place in small town communities, where, at one time, we could all trust just about everyone we met at least to the extent they'd do us no harm; a time when could leave our doors unlocked at night or a window open for a cool breeze or not have to worry about where our children were – or if they'd ever come home again.

In SMALL TOWN MURDER, we will be examining local cases, old cases, more recent cases, and the aftermath it leaves behind for the victim's families – as well as taking an in-depth look into a deep, dark, world none of us would ever want to see – but has been here all along, and, most likely, always will be.